YOU WITHIN ME

A HISTORICAL PARANORMAL ROMANCE

SIMONE BEAUDELAIRE

To all who live in times of fear and uncertainty. It's not bad to escape for a few hours.

ACKNOWLEDGMENTS

I would like to thank my publishers: Next Chapter, the team and especially owner Miika Hannila. Thank you for taking a chance on me. I would also like to thank my dedicated beta reader and dear friend Sandra Martinez, who always asks the hard questions. Finally, I would like to thank my husband, Edwin Stark. He's as good a partner as he is a reader, writer and father.

PROLOGUE

Skeon, a small city-state near the southwestern
border of Egypt's Old Kingdom. 2680 B.C.

*F*ace grim, Leontios stood, his sandals
sinking deep into the thin, muddy soil
outside the wall of Skeon's inner city. With one
hand, he clutched a large scroll. With the other, he
used a chunk of glittering quartz to trace magic
symbols in the air.

"Hurry," Ellani urged. "Hurry. They will be here
soon."

"I'm doing the best I can," he snapped at his
wife. "If you want to help, draw on some of your
moon magic and reinforce what I'm doing."

She grabbed his wrist, and he could feel the

moon energy flowing from the sky, through her and into him. The sun, still lingering on the horizon, energized Leontios. The circuit completed, he murmured, "Me within you."

"You within me," Ellani echoed back.

Together they chanted, "By the power of moon and sun, all things—through us—can be done."

Dim yellow light flared. Leontios didn't need to look to see Ellani illuminate. He didn't need to see his brighter golden glow as the magic of the sun lit him up.

"What are we trying to do?" Ellani asked.

"Conceal the inner city from view," Leontios explained. "My brother cannot defend the outer city —let alone the farms—but we cannot let the Egyptians have the crystal."

"Nor the pool," Ellani agreed. Her voice broke. "Will any of us survive?"

He shook his head. "As slaves," he suggested. "At least, you will. Who knows? Maybe the king's son will become entranced with your beauty and make you his queen."

Ellani sobbed. "I have no heart left to love again."

"I am sorry," Leontios told her, never pausing in the casting of his spell. While it might have seemed an inappropriate moment to have the conversation, he knew he had only a short time to express his regret before the end. "I never wanted to interfere with your family."

"I know you didn't. I wish Kel could have coped with our… relationship. It wasn't your fault."

"Please say you forgive me," Leontios urged. "I may not have intended harm, but harm was done nonetheless."

"I do forgive you." Ellani sniffled. In the extremity of her emotion, power bled from her.

"Easy," Leontios urged. "We may yet survive. Don't give it all away."

"It is not for them," Ellani replied, her words serious as a prophecy despite her continual weeping. "If I live, they may have possession of my body, but my magic will ever be only for Skeon."

Leontios forged one last symbol, and a shimmer of heat rose in the desert. The wall surrounding the inner city gleamed for a moment in gold and yellow, like liquid sand. Then, the glow winked out and the wall itself disappeared.

"Now all we need is the key." Leontios turned to the crystal in his hand.

Shouts rang through the outer city. Bowstrings hummed. Arrows whizzed past.

"Hurry, now, husband." Ellani urged. "Hurry and let us run away into the desert. Let the sun take me, and the moonlit night claim your bones. These Egyptians can never have us."

Another volley whizzed across the outer city.

Ellani choked.

Leontios turned to look. An arrow had entered his wife's back, just beside her spine, traveled through the center of her body, and exited between her ribs. Her eyes opened wide, and she fell in the dust.

Leontios offered a quick prayer for the woman who had been with him for so long. The love they bore for each other—though not as precious to her as that of the mate she'd chosen—still deserved grief. Sadly, there would be no time.

Time. I need more time. No matter what the future holds, we need to stay nearby to tend the crystal.

His wife's moon energy shimmered like moonlight above the ground; her presence not yet departed. Leontios gathered it and tucked it, safe and sound, into the small crystal. It shone faintly blue with her life energy.

Content that he had saved her from both the Egyptians and death itself, Leontios used a blast of sun energy to enhance his power as he tossed the quartz towards the desert beyond and behind the invading enemies.

"My master!" A voice cut into Leontios's dark thoughts. He didn't even turn.

"What is it, Eithon?"

"They have broken through the outer defenses," the young man—Leontios's apprentice—blurted,

4

panting hard. "Please, Master. Do not let them take me. You know how brutally they execute their enemies."

"What do you want, son?" Leontios asked, at last turning away from the now-invisible wall to regard the young man. His shiny black hair dripped with sweat that turned the strands stringy. His tawny face had turned red with fear and exertion, and an embarrassing wet patch marred the front of his trousers.

"Kill me, Master," Eithon begged. "Kill me swiftly and gently. I do not fear death but… but I do fear pain. Don't let them smite me… or worse."

Leontios considered the young man's request. He surely had the ability to end Eithon's life as requested. He reached out and took Eithon's sweaty hand. "The power of the sun flows through me and infuses you. You are now more. Bigger. You belong to the sun. The sun belongs to you. It will protect and save you."

Eithon began to glow. Glow brighter and brighter. For a moment, it seemed as though the sun itself had taken possession of the lad. He glistened, sparkled, and the sparks coalesced into a ball of pure light. Eithon's body, devoid of its life force, collapsed to the dust.

Leontios turned, looking for a convenient object to embed his protégé in.

The shouting and clashing behind him grew

louder. Leontios dared glance over his shoulder. A band of shouting Egyptians waved spears in the air, one adorned with the bloody, gape-mouthed head of his brother, the prince of Skeon.

My time has come to an end.

All around him, his countrymen fell one after another under a hail of arrows and thrusting lances. He could do nothing to save them, and the impotence burned like the desert sun.

So, I am too late, too late to escape. Too late to fight. Like Ellani, I will not live as a slave to the Egyptians.

With his last, failing strength, Leontios opened himself to the final rays of the setting sun. Drawing deeply on his god, he released a burst of sunlight that vaporized enemies, countrymen, and all the houses and gardens of Skeon—everything outside the hidden wall—into dust. He could not save his home, but he would not allow the Egyptians to have it. Now, without most of its landmarks, the oasis would hopefully remain hidden until the threat passed. Until he could return and set things to right.

You are a fool, priest, his reason nagged. *These Egyptians may be gone, but more will come. It will not be safe to enter the oasis for generations. Perhaps centuries. Until then, you are better off unaware like Ellani. And if the crystal finally erupts, you will quietly wink out of existence, unaware.*

The sun sank lower in the horizon, sending a

beam directly into his eyes. Leontios began to glow. His luminescence quickly outpaced the setting sun. The symbols on his scroll lit up with matching intensity. A moment later, his abandoned body dropped into the sand, his scroll beside him.

CHAPTER 1

Athens, 1909

"Violet! Time to go."

Nineteen-year-old Violet Warren sighed and glanced over her shoulder at her father, Hiram, who stood in the doorway of the shop, regarding his ostentatious pocket watch with an air of impatience.

"Just a moment, Father," Violet urged, rubbing her hands together to dispel the gritty dust that had gathered when she touched one fascinating object after another. "I haven't selected my souvenir yet."

"I don't understand," her mother Charlotte said, her head barely visible over Father's shoulder, "why you couldn't find a souvenir in the shops and markets we've already perused. What's so special about this dusty old firetrap?"

The proprietor, who was rearranging vase fragments in the display window at the front of the store, huffed angrily into an oversized mustache.

"Those are tourist trinkets, Mother," Violet said. "I'm not interested in bringing back something made last week and painted to look old."

"Well," Father said, "the boat leaves in two hours whether we're on it or not, and I aim to be on it."

"I understand," Violet agreed, "but I already packed this morning and sent my bags down with the porter. Just give me ten minutes, won't you, please?"

"Five," Father snapped, "and not a moment more."

Rolling her eyes, Violet sneezed out a nose full of dust and peered at the shelf, frantically searching for anything that would bring to mind the marvelous sensations she'd gotten when exploring all those ancient ruins.

At last, something snared her gaze: a patch of tawny leather, mostly concealed behind a shelf full of broken pottery shards. Sliding dull red and vibrant blue ceramic aside, she reached into the depths. She disturbed at least two spiderwebs and left an arm-shaped pattern in the dust before her hand closed around the leather.

Her fingers tingled at the flesh-warm material. She drew it out, brushed off a thick layer of grime and looked at the burnished surface. Now that she could see it more clearly, it resembled nothing so much as human skin. It felt like skin too—thin and ragged—its surface stamped with symbols the likes of which she'd never seen. They resembled a primitive form of Egyptian hieratic, but the symbols did not correspond to any hieratic she'd seen.

Heart pounding, Violet gently eased the cover open. The leather hinges creaked but held. Inside, papyrus sheets, ragged and uneven, contained text in the same strange hieratic along with what seemed to be a set of sophisticated yet primitive drawings like the ones she'd seen in an article about a cave in Spain. Its beauty stole her breath.

"Violet!" Father shouted, "your time is up. Let's go."

Violet inhaled to respond, and a thick cloud of dust rose up, setting her coughing. Closing the book reverently, she carried it to the front of the shop and handed it to the owner so she could dig out her handkerchief and wipe her streaming eyes.

"Would you like to buy this?" the man asked in heavily accented English.

"Yes," Violet replied in even more broken Greek. "How much is it?"

The man quoted a price that made her choke

again, but without reservation, she pulled a roll of dollars out and handed it to him.

Avarice lit the dark eyes. The man grabbed the cash, stroked his beard and extended the book.

Violet grabbed it and ran to the entrance. "I'm ready now, Father," she rasped.

Father regarded the book with a sour expression, twisting his pencil-thin mustache into a frown. "This is what you've dragged me all over Athens to find? You ignored statues, paintings, textiles—anything with any beauty or style—and bought a book. Violet, I fear you'll never find a husband at this rate."

Violet shrugged. "I don't mind."

The boat whistled, its call reverberating across all the buildings in town.

"Let's hurry," Father urged. He took his wife's arm and escorted her across the uneven streets.

"Let's hurry carefully," Mother replied. We still have over an hour to walk only a few blocks. No need to stumble about."

"Yes, I agree," Violet added, her eyes glued to her book, not watching where she was going.

"I will concede your mother's need," Hiram said bluntly to his daughter, "but not yours. You can stare at that damned book for weeks as we sail across the Atlantic. In the meanwhile, step lively. You've dragged your mother around this city more than is good for her in her...cond—"

"Hiram, stop," Charlotte urged. "The doctors say my illness is already under control. It's likely I'll make a full recovery."

Violet heard the false confidence in her mother's voice. *It won't,* she acknowledged sadly. *She weakens every day. This will be our last trip as a whole family. I'm grown, and Mother is...* Her mind veered away from the unwanted thought.

They made their way to the docks and joined a throng of sweating, fretting tourists loading themselves for the long journey home.

This is going to be a long, sad and tiresome trip, Violet thought. *At least I have my book to keep me company.*

CHAPTER 2

Pittsburgh, 1919

"*V*iolet, are you ready? It's almost time to go," Father called from the corridor.

Violet froze, set her book to the side and shoved her foot into her boot. "Almost, Father," she called back.

Hiram knocked on her door and let himself in. "Quit fiddling with that damned book and get ready. You were the one who wanted to go to this party," he groused to his daughter. "The grippe is far from settled, despite the relaxing of quarantine rules. Why would you drag us to a party neither of us wants to go to in the middle of an epidemic?"

"You *should* put in an appearance for the sake of your reputation," Violet pointed out as she tied the

laces into a bow and groped across the bed to retrieve her gauze face mask. "You haven't made
your way so high in your company only to molder
at home as a recluse. Your reputation is based on
your network of supporters. You need to get out
and meet with them sometimes. Besides, no one in
our circles has gotten sick, and you don't even interact with the factory workers anymore. You just
drink tea in the sunroom. Put on a mask, bring a
hankie and go mingle."

"I thought you were going to meet with that
suitor of yours," Hiram rebutted. "I don't need
some slip of a girl telling me how to do my job."

Violet rolled her eyes. "I'm not telling you what
to do. I'm reminding you of what you used to do.
And I don't have a suitor, Father. I hope you don't
mean that idiot you invited to dinner last week. He
didn't even *bring* a hankie. He sneezed all over the
good napkins." She shuddered.

"James Wilson is a good, solid young man. A
rising star in the steel business. I hope we can keep
him, and he doesn't decide to go into competition
against us."

"Hence why you're trying to arrange a reason
for him to stick with the Carnegie corporation?" Violet guessed, rolling her eyes.

Hiram shrugged, creasing his suit coat and his
forehead in a single movement.

A violent sigh tore itself from Violet's chest. "Father, you'll have to find some other incentive to keep Mr. Wilson on board. He's eight years younger than me—too young to be a serious suitor, too old for me to train how to behave properly. That's assuming I wanted to—which I don't. *And* he still thinks he can boss me around. He's definitely not someone I'm interested in."

"You know," Hiram pointed out, "the odds of you finding a man who will let you be the head of the household are extremely low. You should consider whether you ought to compromise that desire rather than be alone. You're no spring chicken."

"Exactly, Father," Violet said. "I didn't reach the great old age of twenty-nine alone by being desperate to find a partner. I'm comfortable being single. If my fate is to become an eccentric spinster, I don't mind. I have quite a special job that I find very fulfilling. I have friends, and I'm not interested in being the head of the household, only an equal partner."

Hiram laughed, though it didn't hold much humor. "Good luck with that, princess. If your mother were here, I'm sure she'd be quick to disabuse you of such nonsense. I have no doubt that, with her guidance, you'd be long married by now. Maybe even a mother."

"What a world," Violet said, intentionally tweaking her father's sensibilities, "where half the population is relegated to only a few of the possible goals, and only the ones that are least respected."

"We're not starting this again," Hiram growled. "Get moving. We're leaving in five minutes."

Frowning, Violet tied the strings of her mask behind the back of her head and plunked a hat on. At the last moment, she grabbed her book, tucked it into her handbag—a large leather satchel heavily decorated with elaborate beading—and headed for the door. *If nothing else, I can hide away in the corner and study these strange hieroglyphics one more time. Maybe different lighting will reveal something I haven't noticed before.*

A sumptuous ballroom hummed with conversation. Drinks flowed freely and luxurious snacks, still rare after years of wartime rationing, adorned several small tables in one corner. Violet suppressed a smile as she watched people eyeing food when they thought no one was looking. *Have to look dignified in the face of chocolate petit fours, filled pastries and rum punch.* It all seemed so artificial. If the party hadn't been hosted by her father's boss, she would have skipped it. *Anything for the family business,* she thought, rolling her eyes. *Hope I don't get the grippe from some idiot coughing in the punch.*

Clutching a cup in her hand as camouflage

against unwanted kindness, her book a comforting weight in her handbag, she moved away from the wall and circulated at random, approaching a crowd and then tiptoeing away.

Randall. Drat. Why does he have to be everywhere I want to go? Her former suiter sported a dashing scar that bisected his left eyebrow. His wild brown hair, which Violet had always loved, had been slicked back with pomade and now looked unnatural. Also greasy. His slim-cut brown suit highlighted a figure that had been transformed by years of hard work overseas from a slender youth to a fuller, more muscular shape.

Women in fancy dresses flocked around him, and he absorbed the adulation with a smug grin that made Violet want to retch.

Good thing I didn't marry him, she thought. *It doesn't look like maturity improved him much.*

Shaking her head, she approached another group.

"Violet," Hiram shouted from the middle of a knot of younger men and women, mostly his work team.

Violet's stomach clenched. "Hello, Father."

"Look who's here."

Violet sighed. "Hello, Mr. Wilson."

"Jim, please," the young man urged. His fingers, their nails bitten to the quick, fluttered as though to smooth his slicked hair, but he ultimately didn't touch. He cleared his throat and coughed but made no move to reach for the hankie in his breast pocket.

Nervous, and no wonder, with Father hovering over his shoulder. Still, nerves are no excuse to spread germs. "How is work?" she asked blandly, not accepting his invitation to use a more intimate name.

"We have fifteen new accounts this month!" the young man exclaimed. Again, he attempted to touch his hair and forced his hand back to his side. "The end of the war didn't hurt business at all! And in spite of the grippe, business is thriving. We're having a hard time containing contagion in the factories because we need so many workers to keep up with demand. They're packed in like sardines."

"How lovely for you," she said sarcastically. *I used to have nothing against the boy, apart from him being too young and too bossy. Now, his casual disregard for suffering doesn't impress me. That makes me even less interested than before.* "If you will excuse me, Father, Mr. Wilson, I must go and greet a friend."

Turning slightly to the side, she meandered away. "This party is boring," she muttered under her breath as she approached the punchbowl. Though more than half the liquid remained in her cup, she added a splash anyway. *Perhaps some alcohol will help smooth the evening.*

"Is everything all right, Miss Warren?" a voice murmured in her ear.

Violet glanced over her shoulder to see the pointy, refined features of her boss, linguistics professor Miles Owen.

"I didn't expect to see you here," she said meekly.

Miles raised one dark eyebrow. "Your father invited me."

"Did he? I wonder why?" Noticing a few cookies on a plate beside the punchbowl, she snagged one and tugged her mask down so she could take a bite. "I would hardly think a bunch of money-grubbing steel tycoons would be interested in world languages."

"On the contrary," the professor protested, "They're always looking for new markets and new customers. Eventually, they will run out of territory in the United States. That means it's important to learn new languages so that they can expand."

"Interesting," Violet said, tucking her mask up around her face. "So, from the realm of pure academia, you've managed to capture the interest of the captains of industry? That's quite a coup."

"I think so," Owen agreed. "I may end up relying on you even more heavily to continue the cataloging and translating of ancient documents, so I can attend to more… profitable matters."

"I'd be delighted," Violet replied. "I'm able to read hieratic without a guide, and my hieroglyphics are almost as good as yours. Do you think, if all goes well in the next year or so, I could get some credit toward the translations?" Snack finished, she tucked the mask up around her face.

"It's possible," Owen said. He ladled himself a glass of the potent punch. "We'll see what the future holds." He downed his drink in a single gulp, coughed, and poured another. It too disappeared quickly.

"Boss, you might want to take it easy on the punch," Violet suggested. "It's pretty strong. You don't want to look bad in front of all these steel tycoons."

Owen raised bushy eyebrows but obediently set his cup down. "So, are you here with anyone?" he asked, fruit and alcohol wafting on his breath. She could smell it right through the gauze of her mask.

"Yes," Violet said.

Owen's face fell.

"With my father," she added.

His dark eyes lit up.

Something in his expression alarmed Violet, and she quickly scooted away from him, muttering a vague excuse in his direction.

Annoyed by the entire party, Violet retreated to the hallway, where late arrivals had long since stopped appearing. Though a lack of windows in this interior space prevented moonlight from reaching her, she found a spot below an electric wall sconce where the light sufficed for her to see her book.

Tugging the ragged, loosely bound volume from her bag, she examined the leathery cover again. With its strange markings of embossed hieratic that she could not read or understand, it frustrated her.

"Someday, I will learn your secrets," she whispered.

The leather seemed to pulse under her fingers. She caressed it.

"Oh, here you are. What do you have there?"

Violet glanced up to see Miles Owen standing beside her. Or rather, leaning. His shoulder rested heavily against the yellow floral wallpaper.

"A book," Violet replied. "I bought it on holiday in Greece several years ago, and I've been trying to read it ever since. Have you ever seen marks like these?"

Carefully and with great reluctance, she extended the volume to her boss.

He examined the cover with narrowed eyes and then opened it with less care than Violet liked. Lips pursing, Owen ran his fingers over the unfamiliar hieratic. Then he shook his head, shut the cover and handed the volume back to Violet. "Looks like you've been rooked, my dear." A soft exhalation and a waft of alcohol seemed to be a burp.

Violet frowned. "What do you mean?"

"That is not a real written language," he replied

bluntly. "It looks like someone bound up a collection of children's scribbles and bound it all in a goat's skin, maybe as a gift for a grandmother. There's nothing to see here. I hope you didn't spend too much on it."

Violet reclaimed the volume and tucked it into her bag without a word. His opinion upset her, but why let that show? *What did you expect, really? You know how he feels about himself. If he doesn't understand something, it must be fake. That's Mr. Owen to the core, and deep down, he knows it, which is why he lets you do the majority of the work while he takes the credit.*

"Miss Warren…"

Violet's head shot up at the tone that had crept into Mr. Owen's voice. "Mr. Owen?"

"Miles, please, Violet."

She raised an eyebrow.

"It was clever of you to step out into the hallway."

She lowered the eyebrow again. Lowered into a posture of suspicion. With her free hand, she groped inside her oversized handbag and fingered the mother-of-pearl inlay on the grip of her derringer. "I wasn't enjoying the party much," she said bluntly. "I wasn't trying to be clever; I was trying to escape the noise."

"As was I," he said. "Since we both wanted to escape the noise, I can think of several quiet things to do to pass the time." He reached out.

She stepped back. "I doubt your wife would approve of this particular pastime."

"As many lovers as she's had, I doubt she'd care," he told her bluntly. "I can assure you I do not."

"I do," Violet replied. "I have no interest in you, Mr. Owen. You're married, and let's not forget that you're also quite full of yourself. I do the work, and you take the glory. What part of that makes you think I'm attracted to you?"

He lurched forward again, lips pursing, hands grasping.

Violet stepped to the side.

Drunk and unbalanced, Mr. Owen stumbled and fell face-first on the floor. A snore emerged.

Violet shook her head. *I hope he doesn't remember this exchange at all. I like my job, and I'd like to keep it a while longer.* Leaving her boss to his booze-induced nap, she stepped back into the annoying party, intent on finding her father and telling him she was going home. *The older I get, the less I enjoy events like these. I should buy a house and host my own parties. I would only invite polite, intelligent people, status be damned. No captains of industry. No egocentric boors. Wouldn't that be nice?*

From inside her bag, her book rested against her thigh, a comforting presence in a room filled with people who wanted to own her without bothering to understand her.

I will never be owned. Never.

~

"He tried to *grab* you?" Marjorie squealed, lowering her mask to show the entirety of her astonished face.

Careful, Violet warned herself, remembering how Marjorie would create interpretations not implicit in the evidence if the story weren't interesting enough. "He *tried*," Violet said, frowning ostentatiously and making sure Esther and Julia were looking. "I told him I wasn't interested in married men about two seconds before he passed out drunk on the floor."

"You should get married," Marjorie said. "The gropy drunks will still be there, but you'd be well within your rights to push them away."

"I already am," Violet pointed out, "and as yet, I haven't found a single man who's worth the trouble. All they want is an ornament to decorate their arm… or a tighter connection with my father. You should see the young fool he's trying to set me up with."

"Is James Wilson really that bad?" Julia asked. "He's quite handsome, and he must earn a decent wage." Settling comfortably into her seat at the table, well-spaced from her friends, she removed her mask, tucked it into her bag and withdrew a han-kie, which she set beside her.

"That is all true," Violet said. "Provided you can countenance his sloppy germ habits. Would you like me to introduce you?"

Julia blushed, revealing her interest.

Excellent. Grinning, Violet sat back in her chair—a ridiculously ornate wooden chair at a ridiculously ornate table covered with a scarlet satin cloth that matched the draperies in Marjorie's dining room. She dropped her purse beside her.

A dimly-lit chandelier flickered overhead, casting mysterious shadows onto the two matrons and two spinsters who had gathered for their fa-vorite diversion—dabbling in spiritualism. Moon-light beamed through several windows—open to the winter cold to increase ventilation—and pro-vided extra illumination.

"Come by for tea someday," Violet urged Julia. "I'll invite him, and you can take him off my hands. That would make everyone happy."

"Everyone except your father," Marjorie pointed out.

Violet shrugged. "He has spent his whole life doing exactly what he wanted, despite his immi-grant parents not understanding it. He made a for-tune, gained an influential position in a very important company and everything. I get to choose my own path, even if he doesn't understand it."

"Perhaps," Esther suggested, snotty as usual, "he objects to providing for a relative who refuses to do what she needs to do to and creates a financial burden on him for her own selfish gain."

Violet raised an eyebrow at Esther, silently challenging her rudeness. "That's inaccurate, and you know why, but never mind. I don't need to explain again. My life is not yours to determine either, even if you don't understand it."

"You see," Esther commented to the room, confident as a preacher in a pulpit, "how she refuses to defend herself?"

"I see," Julia spoke up, uncharacteristically bold in the face of disapproval, "that you've set Violet a trap. In your estimation, refusing to defend herself to you—and you have no authority over her, so she has no need to do so—confirms that you're right. Last time, when she did attempt to explain herself, you shot down her reasons. I don't think you care at all about Violet, only about imposing your views. It's an odd choice given that we've dedicated ourselves to finding and considering all the world's truths."

"One lazy spinster to another," Esther snarked. "If you search the world around, you'll find one inescapable truth: a woman needs a man. A woman without a man is a burden."

Violet laughed. "That may be your truth, Esther, but it's not mine, and I doubt it's as universal as you think. Regardless, since I don't answer to you, I think we'd better drop the subject. We're here to see who Marjorie brought to enlighten us, not to argue amongst ourselves."

Esther scowled, creating deep grooves around her mouth. Though only a few years older than Violet, she had already begun her transformation into a prudish old crone.

She never stops promoting marriage, even though hers is far from happy. I'd rather be a spinster with an education, a job and as much freedom as our society allows a woman than be saddled to a controlling and violent man.

Sometimes, she thought she might be protesting too much.

"So, Marjorie," she turned to her host, shaking off unsettling thoughts, "what medium have you found today? Will we have another séance?"

Marjorie scoffed. "After the way you chased away my last medium, no one else will come. This is something different."

Violet raised her eyebrows. "Well, if you'd stop employing charlatans, it would be better."

Marjorie sighed. "Violet, I don't know if they're charlatans until we try them, but if you would give them a chance…"

Violet laughed. "I do. It's just that… some are so terrible." Then, she realized what she was doing—carrying her quarrel with Esther to Marjorie, who was not responsible for it. "But of course, you wouldn't know that either and charlatans need to make a living too. All right, I'll try to be kind to your… entertainers in the future."

"At least for a little while," Marjorie replied, grinning. "If they're terrible, you're welcome to say something… once we've gotten our money's worth."

Violet grinned back just as a light tap sounded at the door of the comfortable parlor into which a table and chairs had been introduced.

"Ma'am?" One of Marjorie's many maids poked her head in the door.

"Yes, Sarah?"

"Your… guest… is here to see you." The young woman puckered her lips with disapproval.

"Show him in," Marjorie urged.

The young maidservant took a step back from the door, and then she scuttled away. With a stately step, a strange, short figure strode into the room. Clad in a robe of brilliant blue adorned with glittering metallic stars, a pointed velvet hat and blue velvet shoes that curled up at the toes, the stranger approached the table and seated himself with a flourish in the empty chair, staring at the group with half-lidded blue eyes. "I am the Great Marvolo," the man intoned in an oddly high-pitched voice.

"Welcome, Marvolo," Marjorie replied in her

perfectly modulated hostess voice. "What do you have to share with us tonight?"

From her seat beside the mystic, Violet examined the man closely. Something about the stubble on his lip and chin, the shape of his features, the curve of his portly lower belly struck Violet as odd.

"I am here to show you the wonders of the universe," Marvolo proclaimed. "The mysticism and magic of long-dead civilizations. Ancient knowledge lost to modern man!"

"That tells us a lot," Violet murmured, trying to contain her desire to snicker. "Do you have any *substance* to add to that claim?"

Marvolo stuck out his lips.

Violet narrowed her eyes. "You're not a man at all, are you," she blurted.

Marjorie grunted and leaned over, poking her in the ribs.

"I'm sorry," Violet said, not in the least bit contrite, "but she's not. Look at her."

The mystic scowled.

"Come now," Violet urged. "How do you expect us to trust your otherworldly knowledge if you aren't even honest about your identity?"

"I can tell you your past, present and future," the strange creature intoned, sweeping a loose strand of curly black hair off her forehead.

Violet laughed. "Go right ahead, but listen, Great Marvolo, I'd still like you to wipe the cosmetics off your chin. The false beard is distracting me.

Marvolo sighed. Gathering up a big handful of her loose blue robe, she smeared at the carefully drawn stubble, leaving a dark brown smudge. "Better?" she demanded, her voice suddenly feminine and possessed of a New England accent. "Yes, I'm a woman, all right? My name is Layla. I've had some problems with clients who didn't respect me because I'm not male. I really do have insights, though. Also, a Syrian grandmother who has given me access to some pretty interesting objects I'd like to show you."

"For sale?" Violet guessed.

"Of course." Marvolo raised one eyebrow and then tossed off her hat to reveal short-cropped curly hair that stood in a thick bush around her ears.

Now that the mystic showed signs of being honest, Violet relaxed, ready to appreciate her spiel. "All right, Marvolo. Impress me."

The woman grinned. "I'll start with you then since you seem to be the resident skeptic."

Violet shrugged. "I'm willing to be convinced. I just object to being manipulated. Show me what you can do."

"Tall order. Very well. You're a strong woman. A woman who's not afraid to break boundaries if you see the value in doing so. You want a future where you are respected more than you want the illusion of love, but love is waiting for you."

Violet raised her eyebrow. "You think so?"

"Yes. Your lion. Strong, but not overbearing. He's waiting where you least expect but most want to find him." The woman lowered her eyebrows in deep contemplation. "Together, you will do something so important it could change… change so much. Improve so much… It's blocked. I'm not permitted to see what it is you will be saving, but…" she shook her head. "You will hesitate, but if you do not ultimately reject closeness in favor of independence, there will be great rewards for you and for the world."

"Interesting," Violet murmured, not sure what to make of the prediction.

"Oh, and you need this too." Reaching inside her robe, Marvolo pulled out a chunk of highly polished white quartz consisting of a faceted base and three projecting points, each one seeming to aim in a slightly different direction. The pale moonlight flashed in the crystal's depth and pale rainbows danced on the opposite wall.

"It's beautiful," Violet breathed, extending her hand. At that moment, nothing could have seemed more appealing than holding that chunk of shining crystal. The moment it touched her palm, a shock went through her. It felt… it felt… "Alive!" she breathed.

"What do you mean?" Esther demanded, suspicious as always.

"Yes," Marjorie agreed. "How can a chunk of rock be alive? What do you mean alive?"

Violet shook her head. "I don't know exactly. It's like…" she leaned forward, and the electric sensation of the crystal faded. She blinked. "It's gone. What is this, Marvolo?"

"I don't know," the mystic admitted. I get wholesale boxes of junk from several small sellers I happened to meet while visiting my mother's family. Most of it is chunks and shards of ancient pottery. This crystal came with some jars and part of a statue covered in symbols I'd never seen before. Somehow, I knew I needed to bring it tonight. Perhaps it was asking to come for you."

"Perhaps it was," Violet murmured, finally willing to be impressed by the Great Marvolo.

Unison gasps revealed her friends' shock at her sudden credulity, but Violet didn't care. The sparkling crystal spoke to her in ways she couldn't understand. All she knew was she wanted it. She shifted in her chair, and a shaft of moonlight shone through the blinds of Marjorie's parlor window and hit the rock again. Tingles shot up Violet's arm and set her shoulders buzzing. *I will not leave without this crystal, no matter the cost,* she thought dreamily.

"Well, since you've won over your skeptic," Marjorie said, irony thick in her well-modulated voice, "how about me? Do you have any fascinating prognostications for your host?"

Violet glanced away from her riveting acquisition to see Marjorie's eyebrow raised in a way that revealed growing grooves on her face.

"Well," Marvolo said, suddenly sounding timid, "I hate to tell you, but you'll never have a child."

Marjorie gasped.

"Sorry to be so blunt. It's not you. It's your husband. He's incapable. Don't worry, though. You'll find many ways to bring light to the world. There will be some pain as you adjust, but in the end, you'll be satisfied with your legacy."

Marjorie grunted.

"As for you," the strange woman turned to Esther, "your path is clouded. If you quickly learn to temper your unkindness, your future is bright. If you persist in being a rude, harsh gossip, you'll lose everything you love. Friends, children, until only your husband is left. And you know what will happen if he isolates you completely. Think carefully about whether the petty enjoyment you get from attacking your friends and family is worth more than their presence in your life."

Esther hissed and rose from her chair. "I don't have to listen to this garbage," she snarled, storming toward the door.

"Have a care," Marvolo urged. "You came to ask the question. Don't reject the answer. It will make the difference between dying happy, surrounded by your loved ones, or dying alone with the beast that torments you."

Esther didn't pause in her mad rush for the door.

Julia giggled. "You're good at this. What about me?"

The Great Marvolo turned, her wicked smile dying to sorrow. "I'm so sorry, my dear." She reached for Julia and patted her hand. "Your future is very short."

Julia choked. "What do you mean?"

Marvolo nodded. "I think you already know."

Julia's eyes pinched, and her hand fluttered toward her belly. "Can I do anything?"

Marvolo shook her head. "What you're planning won't help you. This is meant to be."

Julia gulped, and her lower lip quivered.

"Do not attempt to escape your fate. It will only make things worse for you—"

"That's enough," Marjorie snapped. "I brought you here to entertain us, not to hurt everyone's feelings."

Marvolo raised her eyebrows, which she'd drawn in thickly to resemble something bushy and masculine. "Sometimes, the truth hurts. I didn't realize you wanted fake readings to giggle over."

"You should leave now." Marjorie rose from her seat and pointed to the door.

Marvolo sighed. "Very well. I'll need that." She snatched the crystal out of Violet's hand and turned toward the door. "I'll be back tomorrow to receive the payment you've promised me. Do not try to cheat me, madam. I am not easily put off."

Marjorie snorted.

No sooner did the door swing shut behind Marvolo than Violet was out of her chair and bolting after the woman, ignoring her friends' shouts of surprise.

In the hallway, she found Marvolo waiting.

"I expected you," the woman stated plainly.

"I'm sure you did."

"I'm sure you want to know why I didn't tell you about your fate, right?"

"Yes." Violet crossed her arms over her chest and leaned against the wall.

"That's because I don't know." In the dim light of the overhead chandelier, the woman's face looked both mysterious and perplexed. "I've never seen anything like you, Violet Warren. Your future is so clouded. It's not certain, like your friend Julia, who will die in the next year, or your friend…" this time, irony dripped from her voice as she pronounced the name, "who will die by the hand of her violent husband, hated by everyone. Even your friend Marjorie, who cannot choose to have a child, but who can choose to be happy with what she has or miserable with what she lacks. Your destiny is different."

Violet raised one golden brown eyebrow.

"I could tell you a story about a mysterious stranger and a journey across the sea, but I doubt that would impress you. Instead, I will suggest that whatever you do in the next year or so, you take *that* book with you. The book and the crystal, which I will have to insist you pay for before we part ways."

Violet stood up straight. "What do you know about my book?"

"I told you I have the sight. You can believe me and keep your book close, or you can leave it behind and run the risk of being caught unprepared in a situation I cannot warn you about."

Violet thought about this. Thought about it for a long time. So long, in fact, that Marvolo began to tap the strange toe of her embroidered shoe on the floorboards.

"How much?" she asked at last.

Marvolo's grin nearly split her face in two.

CHAPTER 3

"What's that you've got there?" Violet's father demanded.

Violet looked up from her seat in the parlor. Sunlight beamed through the window through her new trident-shaped prism onto one of the pages of her book. The rainbows highlighted a patch of scribbly hieratic. It looked pretty, but it did nothing to reveal the meaning.

Then, Hiram Warren's shadow fell across the page, erasing the colored bands of light.

"Nothing in particular," Violet replied. "Why do you ask?"

"No reason."

Violet perceived the note in her father's voice. She scrutinized his face, looking for more information. "What's bothering you?"

"Just a rumor I heard."

She raised an eyebrow. "You've taken to listening to rumors?"

"Only when they come from certain people."

"Who?"

"Oh, Jim. You know, my protégé?" Hiram sank into an armchair and crossed one leg over the opposite knee.

Violet sighed and gently closed the cover of her book. "What does Jim have to say for himself?"

"That he saw you in the hallway at the party, alone with your employer, and it didn't look… seemly."

Violet shook her head. "Yes, Miles Owen was there. You invited him, remember? I went to the hallway mainly to escape him. He'd had too much to drink, and yes, he was behaving in an unseemly way. That is, until he passed out from drink, and I left for the evening."

Hiram frowned. "And yet, you've gone to work with him every day this week."

Violet shrugged. "It's one of the reasons I don't like to go to these parties. Everyone acts differently when the pressure is off and the alcohol flows, and it's usually unsettling. Time will tell if Prohibition—once it goes into effect—makes a difference in women's safety. In the meanwhile, Mr. Owen has far more to lose than I do if he misbehaves. Besides, he doesn't act that way at work."

"But you keep working with him, even after he behaved so badly?"

Violet shrugged. "I like my job. Where else can I put my multilingual reading ability to use?"

"I do wish you had chosen a more ladylike hobby," Hiram mumbled.

"It's not a hobby, Father," Violet reminded him, "any more than selling steel is your fun way to relax on the weekend. It's my profession. I think you've forgotten—again—that I am not some useless trinket who lives on tea and gossip. You might prefer that, but it will never be. Can you accept it, or is it time for me to seek a home of my own?"

"Alone," Hiram muttered, mostly to himself.

"Yes, alone," Violet confirmed. "I haven't yet met anyone I would want to share a home with, and before you ask, I wouldn't marry Jim Wilson if he was the last man on earth. I've told you that before. I have a friend who might like to meet him."

"I don't understand why the very thought of marriage makes you so uncomfortable, Violet. You're an… an interesting person. You're intelligent and quirky, and you still look rather pretty. Someone would surely like you well enough to take the plunge."

"That person would have to take me on as I am," Violet replied, gently this time. "Not in hopes of currying favor with you. Not demanding I be his housekeeper, bedwarmer and doily maker."

Hiram sputtered at Violet's frank confession, but she continued anyway. "I'm a trained linguist and translator of ancient documents. That means more to me than the promise of a staff of servants to command and a slew of children to bring up."

Hiram frowned. "Out of all the offspring I might have had, I got the strangest one."

Violet laughed. "You did. At least, the strangest daughter. If I had been a son?"

"You'd still be strange, but I think it would be easier to understand."

Setting her book on the end table, Violet reached across to pat her father's hand. "Then don't worry about understanding. Can't you just accept me for who I am?"

He nodded. "I always have, haven't I? I may make suggestions, but I haven't forced anything on you."

"That is true, and I appreciate your forbearance."

The pair fell silent.

"Do you know something?" Hiram said.

"What's that, Father?"

"I feel restless. We used to travel so much. Every year or two."

"I remember. I always cherished those trips."

"As did I. As did your mother. I think…" his voice wavered. "I think she would like to know we didn't give up our tradition of seeing the world."

41

"And now that the war is over, and the grippe seems to be waning—at least abroad…"

"Yes," he agreed. "Where would you like to go?"

Violet smiled. "Egypt. I've always wanted to see the source of all those artifacts I've been translating and cataloging. I was afraid—with the war raging and Spanish Flu mopping up everyone that was left —that I'd never get a chance to visit the pyramids. Do you think we can get paperwork approved to travel out of the country? Between the passport act and the quarantines, they'll want a very good reason to let us out."

"I'm sure I can make it happen," Hiram said. "If I say it's for business, everything else should fall in line, and it won't cost me more than a couple of conversations with local leaders of industry."

"Perfect."

CHAPTER 4

"*V*iolet, come along!" Hiram exclaimed, the polished toe of his boot tapping in the street at the entrance of yet another store filled with junk and antiquities. "We're going to miss the train."

"You should change your shoes," she replied mildly. "Those fancy things won't last a day in the desert."

"The train," he reminded her.

Violet sneezed into a handkerchief, waved a cloud of dust away from her face and regarded her father through watering eyes. "The train leaves in two hours. Our luggage is being loaded for us at the station. I may not get another chance to see Alexandria, so I'm not missing out. If you don't want to be here, go get a cup of tea, but I'm not leaving yet."

Resolutely, she returned her attention to the shelves in front of her. Places like this, with their jumbles of broken pottery and piles of goatskin scrolls, never failed to fire her blood. Here, also, most of the merchandise was written in Arabic which, though she could read it, wasn't her true goal.

Her blood tingled in her veins the way it always did when something truly ancient crossed her path. It was why she had gone into her line of work. Why her bedroom bristled with inscribed pottery shards and crumbling papyri. *And it's why I'll never marry,* she added, peering through a cluster of broken junk in search of hidden treasures. *Any reasonable husband would want me to, at the very least, organize the servants and make a home. All I want is to learn new languages and translate old documents, and if I don't want to fall into crippling sorrow, I must allow myself to continue.*

Continue she did. Clutching her hankie to her mouth and nose to minimize the dust, she peered into every corner of the dusty shop. The prickling sensation strengthened as she reached the corner of the room, where several large pots and a few Roman-style amphorae lay on their sides in a cluster of uncomplimentary colors.

Violet stared at the mishmash, one eyebrow

down, squinting for the source of her intuitive attraction. Among the pots, a small, flat disc of fired
clay lay forgotten. The moment Violet saw it, her
heart began to pound. The symbols on the left side,
beside a line of raised clay, were Egyptian hieratic,
and she immediately understood them. The symbols on the right…

"Oh, my word," she breathed. Scooping up the
disc, she made her way to the clerk. "What is this?"
she asked in Arabic.

A small, dark-haired man with handsome features grinned at her wolfishly. "I don't know,
ma'am," he said.

Violet narrowed her eyes at him, warning him
not to get too familiar, even as his obvious interest
sparked warmth in her belly. "Would you like me to
take it off your hands?"

He shrugged, making his brown eyes wide and
innocent. "For a price."

"Naturally," Violet agreed. "I'll pay a small price
for it. I mean, if you don't know what it is, it can't
be worth much to you, right?"

The wide eyes narrowed, and a sneaky look
crossed the man's face. "True, but I can see it means
something to you."

"Perhaps," Violet said, giving the man her own
wide-eyed nonchalance. "I like strange things. This
one is pretty. How much do you want for it?"

"How much are you willing to pay?"

She examined the disc again. "One hundred Egyptian pounds," she replied firmly, offering an equivalent of about ten dollars, which she knew was low for an ancient artifact, even a small one of an unknown origin.

"Five hundred," he replied.

She shook her head. "Maybe if it was verifiably Ancient Egyptian," Violet said. "I can see the hieratic here, but this other writing… it's not. This could easily be a prank. Two hundred. That's my final offer."

He frowned. "You're trying to rob me. Think of my poor children."

"Do you have children?"

He laughed. "Someday, I may."

Violet couldn't help but laugh along with him. "Two-twenty… that jest was worth something to me."

"Agreed." He extended his hand, and they shook. His touch sent an interesting sensation up her arm, and the warm, gentle mischief in his eyes sent it deeper. How long had it been since she'd been attracted to anyone? And why this man? He did have Violet's favorite combination of warm brown eyes—complete with crinkles in the corners —and dark hair, with a neat beard.

His expression turned considering. "Will you be in town long, Miss?" he asked as she handed him the money.

"Sadly, no," Violet replied, her gaze lingering on the attractive gentleman. "I'm boarding a train shortly."

"Ah, yes. That's what your father said. What a pity."

"Violet!" As if on cue, Hiram reappeared in the doorway of the shop, his face red with heat and irritation.

"I'm coming," she replied with a sigh. "I didn't realize you understood English," she added to the shopkeeper. "Why didn't you admit it right away?"

"Your Arabic was rusty," he quipped, eyes twinkling. "I wanted to give you the chance to practice."

"Rusty!" Violet feigned outrage.

He chuckled. "Better move along, Miss. It was lovely to work with you. The next time you're in Alexandria…"

"I promise to annoy my father by spending time and money in your shop," she replied.

He grinned.

As Violet made her way out of the shop, her prize clutched to her chest, she reflected on the encounter. *That meaningless flirtation with an Arab shopkeeper moved me more than any of the suitors my father has sent my way. I wonder what it means. Am I not attracted to men of my own race then? Or is it just that Egypt is so magical?*

If her first guess was correct, she was in for a lot of trouble.

"What did you find this time?" Hiram asked.

"A document on a pottery disc," she replied. "It seems to be a translation guide, similar to the Rosetta stone. I noticed some Egyptian hieratic on it, so I bought it. Might be useful for work." Somehow, explaining to her father that it reminded her of the book that so annoyed him didn't seem wise.

The two walked through Alexandria at a pace too fast for Violet's comfort. "Father, we don't need to rush," she urged. "There's still over an hour until our departure. We might not get another chance to see Alexandria. What's the hurry?"

"We're here to see the pyramids, not this dusty berg," Hiram shot back.

"This 'dusty berg' was built during the reign of Alexander the Great and is historically important in many ways," Violet argued. "We could as easily adventure here as Cairo."

Hiram grunted and trotted on.

They arrived at the train station. Hurrying through the building past a rainbow of people wearing everything from suits to dungarees to robes, Violet wrinkled her nose at the body odor. The heat of the setting sun made it inevitable, but she still found it unpleasant.

Remember that adventures inevitably have their discomforts—and that most of the world's interesting places are hot and therefore smelly. Grinning at herself, she fitted her mask over her face and followed her father up onto the train. They made their way to their compartment.

"Well," Violet said, "we leave in forty-five minutes. Now what?"

"Now, I will go and get myself a cup of tea," he replied.

Violet rolled her eyes. "Rather than getting your tea in town and letting me shop, you decided to rush me back to the train, so we can sit here with nothing to do *except* drink tea. Father, why do I travel with you?"

"Because you're not married," Hiram replied, eyebrow raised. "So, since you're a spinster, you have to put up with my old-man idiosyncrasies. Besides, you're just going to read that damned book anyway."

Violet laughed but with much less amusement than she felt towards the shopkeeper. *Perhaps because he's my father and he's bossed me my whole life. Perhaps because, at nearly thirty, I do sometimes wonder what I'm missing. Not enough to settle for anything that comes along, but enough to consider the prospects.*

Various intimate parts of her anatomy, still humming from the teasing encounter with the shopkeeper, reminded her that just because she was a reasonable creature did not mean she lacked human drives.

Hiram sauntered out of the compartment and did not return.

49

Violet forgot about him almost immediately, excited as she was by her new find.

Hurriedly, she laid the disc on the seat beside her before rummaging in her handbag for her book.

As she dug deep to get a grip on the fragile tome, her fingers brushed against the crystal. It felt warm and cool at the same time, and it tingled against her skin. She stroked it with the tip of her index finger before retrieving her prize. Setting it beside the pottery disc, she stared at the cover. Sure enough, the symbols matched the cover of the book. The symbols corresponded one to one with the hieratic.

"I can translate you," she breathed. "I will learn your secrets."

Swallowing hard against a rush of emotion, Violet almost didn't notice when the train lurched to a start. She traced the complex pattern of etch marks and insect and flower ink on the leather cover and compared them with the document she'd just purchased, voicing the words aloud with the best pronunciation research could find.

"Book of spells. High Priest of the Sun. Brother to the Prince of Skeon…" She traced the cartouche that finished the line "Leontios."

Gently, she traced her fingertips over the words again. "Leontios. Who were you? It says brother to the prince, so royal. High priest, so spiritual. Interesting." Then, she realized what she was saying.

"Interesting and dead for millennia. Don't get excited about this, Violet. The shopkeeper was a better prospect. At least he has a pulse."

Still, she couldn't drag her eyes away from the book, except to double-check her newly purchased guide. "Well, Leontios, let's see what you have to say for yourself."

The shadows deepened as the sun sank lower in the sky.

She turned the page and read, word by word, translating as she went. "Me within you… you within me… By the power of…. moon and… sun, all things in us… can be done."

The train shuddered violently, throwing Violet from her seat. She fell forward, hitting the opposite seat and falling sideways against the wall, her head knocking the window hard. Lights flashed behind her eyelids. Loud booms and shouts filtered into the compartment. Violet curled into a ball as the train continued to lurch, brakes screaming.

A hand came down on Violet's arm.

She screeched, eyes flying open to see… boots. Strange, primitive leather boots with laces up the front that looked like strips of rabbit fur. She lifted her eyes up the length of a body—a slim, wiry male body clad in buff-colored trousers that hung strangely under a loose shirt that also laced up the front with a simple strip of leather—to a face.

Medium brown skin. A tidy goatee. High cheek-bones. Piercing black eyes.

The man had tattoos at his temples, streaks of purple. More dotted his neck and chest where the openings of his shirt revealed his skin. Also, his hands and forearms.

Violet recoiled, but the train's wall prevented her from escaping.

She was trapped.

The man opened his mouth and uttered a string of words Violet felt she could almost recognize, though she couldn't place the words at the speed with which he spoke them.

"Who are you?" she demanded. "What do you want? Why are you in my compartment? My father will be back any moment."

The man tilted his head, clearly not understanding. He reached out with one hand toward Violet as though to help her to her feet.

She stared at him, stunned to see a terrorist offering a helpful gesture. *He must want to get his hands on me so he can take me hostage,* she thought, trying again, helplessly, to escape through the metal plate of the train wall.

The man jabbed his hand in her direction, his dark eyes wide and gentle. They shone black, like chips of obsidian, glinting with intelligence.

Something in Violet wanted to trust him, at least enough to let him help her up. *If he turns threaten-*

ing, I can try to escape better on my feet than huddled in a corner. She knew she was unlikely to escape. Of course, the train had been attacked. She, as a moderately-statured American woman, would stand out too much to slip away unnoticed. She was also too weak to fight back. Her heart pounded, acknowledging her likely fate, but her busy mind was not ready to accept defeat.

She slowly extended her hand, and he grasped her fingers gently. A tingle ran up her arm. *What's wrong with you?* She demanded as the stranger applied slight pressure to her hand, easing her up from the floor.

She rose, eyes darting to the opening behind her in search of any means of escape.

The man spoke again, the words even more familiar than before. As though she had said them herself at some point.

More heat tingled up her arm, not gently this time but with the intensity of a fire. It hurt. She whimpered.

Another bright light flashed, and Violet closed her eyes. A confused tangle of images flared inside her mind. The symbols from her book. The desert at sunrise. A clash of spears on shields. Horses running. Water running. A crystal the size of a car. More symbols. The moon.

Violet sank to her seat, dizzy, the train invasion forgotten. Fabric swished as the stranger released her hand. She opened her eyes and looked up at him. "What *are* you?" she demanded in Arabic.

He lowered his eyebrows, reaching for her again.

"No!" Violet recoiled again. Though more yielding than the wall, the upholstered seat still provided her no escape. "Don't touch me!"

"Please," he said in heavily accented English, accented with… she knew not what. "Please do not be afraid. I will not harm you."

She blinked. "Who are you?"

"I am Leontios," he replied, laying his hand on his chest. "High priest of the sun, brother to the king… He was once the king of Skeon."

"What in the world are you talking about?" Violet demanded.

The heavy, dark brows came together. The man opened his mouth to speak.

Another reverberating crash shook the train. This time they jolted sharply to the right. Leontios stumbled against the interior wall of the compartment with Violet sprawled on top of him. Shouts in Arabic rang through the corridor, and screams answered.

"Oh, no," Violet whispered. "We're under attack." Then she realized what she had said. *Fool, he's one of them.*

"Stay low," the man growled. "Keep quiet."

"Obviously," Violet snapped in an undertone,

rolling off the strange man and trying not to blush at all the different parts of their anatomy that had no business touching. Staying at ground level, she peeked out into the corridor to see many sets of feet rushing towards them and ducking into various compartments. The shouts and screams intensified as they drew near her.

"Move!" Leontios snarled.

Violet shook her head, drawing back into the compartment to grab her satchel, which she slung diagonally across her body. The crystal hung in a heavy weight to the floor, clunking softly against her derringer. She took one last second to stuff in the translation disk, but of her book, she could find no sign.

"Where is it?" she whispered, heart panging at the thought of abandoning her years-long companion. If she left without it, she knew she'd never see it again.

"Come *on*!" Leontios dragged her back toward the door. "Stay low," he hissed. He edged up to the doorway and peeked out, jumping back quickly. Again, the shouting voices drew closer, but they hadn't reached them. Not yet.

"Now!" Leontios pulled Violet into the hallway. "How do we get out of this… structure?"

She raised an eyebrow he couldn't see. *How did you get in?* she thought but didn't waste time arguing. "This way," she hissed, moving quickly, hunched over beneath her unexpected companion's slim chest. The exit to the car waited a dozen or so steps down the hallway. Without waiting a moment, she darted for the door, praying in every language she knew that no guard would be posted to bar their way.

Despite his height, Leontios's feet fell softly on the metal plate beneath them. He swished more than stomped, right at Violet's heels. Time seemed to bend, the corridor stretching as the door retreated farther with every step they took.

"Hurry," she breathed. "Hurry."

Suddenly, the exit loomed before her. Grabbing a slender vertical metal pole, Violet pivoted and stumbled down a step to a closed door. She pushed with all her might. It inched open as Leontios collided with her back, shoving them both through.

A voice shouted behind them. A loud explosion sounded. A projectile crashed into the wall above them and shattered. Hot fragments rained down, one hitting Violet's calf, just above her boot. She bit her lip to contain a scream as she scrambled forward.

Leontios shot to his feet, dragged her upright, and ran away from the train, perpendicular to the tracks. They crested a small rise and dropped flat into the sand.

Back at the train, voices shouted in Arabic.

"What are you doing, Ajnabi?"

"Some people ran toward the hill."

"Let them go. We have enough hostages."

"But…"

"If you leave this train, Ajnabi, you won't be allowed back. You've disobeyed enough orders already."

Boots stomped away.

Violet sagged, resting her forehead on the dusty ground, eyes tightly closed to prevent sand from blinding her. The crisis past, sobs burned their way up her throat. Her shoulders heaved. Her calf throbbed.

"Hush," her strange companion said, not harshly, but as a soothing sound. "Hush, woman. We are safe now." His hand landed gently on her back and rubbed in a circle.

She struggled to regain her composure, biting hard on her lip. Though the worst of the danger may be behind them, the full impact of the situation slowly grew in her awareness. *Father.* He had never come back from the dining car. Had he escaped? Been taken? Injured? Worse? Her book. Luggage. All her possessions. All she had was her handbag with its two pieces of esoteric and utterly useless junk, some money and her travel documents. A sip of brandy in her father's fancy flask to counter the burning sun. The feeling of utter helplessness choked her, setting her off again.

"What is it?" Leontios had drawn close, his breath warm and soft against the side of her face.

She sniffled. "My father. My father is on the train."

His stroking hand stilled, a warm press between her shoulder blades that somehow melted the tension building within her. "That is sad, but is he not an old man? Is it common in this place to target the elderly?"

"Not specifically, no," she admitted, trying to take comfort in the words, "but they attacked the train. The one called Ajnabi tried to shoot us."

"And the other held him back. I suspect they are trying to make a statement rather than an attack."

"Are they?" Wiping her eyes, Violet leaned up on one elbow and challenged him with a probing stare. "Are you one of them? A rebel Egyptian? Did you disobey orders for some reason and steal me away for your own purposes?"

Leontios sat straight up. His dark head came level with the top of the small hill. His full lips compressed, and Violet could hear his teeth grinding. "I am *not* Egyptian," he hissed. "They are my enemies as well as yours. I saved you from them. Do you want them to smite you?"

Violet laughed, and it sounded bitter. "Are you joking? Smite me? I'm worried they might *shoot* me… along with a myriad of other unpleasant fates, some of them specific to women. What a bizarre thing to say. Do you think that will persuade me to trust you?"

Leontios's eyes narrowed. "Shoot?"

"With a *gun*," Violet drawled. "Didn't you notice the bullet? It hit my leg."

"I do not know what that means. Are you injured?"

She nodded. "I think it's bleeding, but it's not bad." Twisting around, she lifted the hem of her skirt and examined the injury. "More like a scratch than a bullet wound, fortunately. I hope I don't get an infection. But what do you mean you don't know what it means? Where have you been that you don't know what a gun is? A bullet?"

"Where I have been, you would not believe. However, you *can* believe that we share an enemy. It seems that these Egyptians have continued their warlike ways and are as treacherous as they ever were. If we can trust each other, perhaps we can find our way to safety, though I admit I do not know where such a place might be."

Violet regarded Leontios suspiciously. Though his demeanor seemed sincere, his words made little sense. "I believe you are not Egyptian," she said at last. "You said Skeon, right? I've never heard of it but given how primitive your understanding of modern weapons is, perhaps it's remote and not well-known outside the Middle East."

Leontios shook his head. "Too many words. Too

little context. I do not understand. I should be able to speak your language."

Violet lowered her eyebrows. "How *do* you speak my language? You don't know Arabic, the language of your neighbors and enemies, but you know my language, which originates halfway around the world?"

Leontios smiled, and the wicked curving of his sensual lips and the twinkle of his dark eyes skewered Violet's guts like a spear, pinning her in place. *This man is dangerous.*

"It's magic," he said smugly.

CHAPTER 5

$\mathcal{V}$iolet's head dropped. "Magic. Of course. That's all it needed. I must be dreaming." Her scrape burned, belying her assertion. "Well, here we are. So, you're Leontios. Same as the name on my book. You do magic. That's how you learned English in one second. You're not Egyptian. I must have hit my head harder than I thought when the train stopped. Now I'm hallucinating. Wake up, Violet."

She pinched herself.

It hurt.

Damn. Guess I'll have to play along until I wake up. "Leontios, my name is Violet Warren. I'm from Pittsburgh, Pennsylvania and I'm here in Egypt on vacation. That's why I was on the train."

He shook his head again. "Too many words.

These must be ideas I do not understand. What is a train?"

Violet raised both eyebrows so high, it felt like they would touch her hairline. "A train? Are you serious?"

He regarded her steadily.

"A train is like a conveyance."

His face compressed. "Conveyance. A structure with wheels. Like a chariot or cart."

"In this case, more like several carts strung together. They run along a track…" She paused, waiting to see how he would process this.

"A path?" he asked.

"It's a set of metal rails. The wheels must remain on the tracks."

He contemplated. "So, the metal structure we left… this is the train?"

"Yes," Violet agreed. "It moves between the cities of Alexandria and Cairo. Or it did. Once the train is off the rails," she peeked over the hill and pointed to the engine of the train, which no longer rested on the tracks but lay on its side in the dust, "it's stuck. It won't move again. Many people will be needed to turn it upright. It's lucky I was so far back, or I might have been injured." Then she remembered her bizarre experiences. "Worse than I already am. I could be dying right now. The dining car is further forward. I'm worried about my father."

"This is your world, not mine, VioletWarren," Leontios said. "How can we help him?"

Despite her still-pounding heart, his address struck her as humorous. "Just Violet will do. Warren is... my family name. Similar to how you named yourself in relation to your brother."

Leontios pursed his lips as he pondered her words. Then he dipped his chin in acknowledgment. "I think I understand. Violet then. It would seem that the two of us, without weapons, would not be very effective against the troublemakers inside the... train. Do you agree? If we march back in and demand they return your father..."

Violet rolled her eyes. "We would find out what happened to him, yes, but we would probably join him as hostages."

"Egyptians do not take hostages," Leontios snapped, suddenly annoyed. "They smite their enemies and take the rest as slaves."

Violet smiled sadly. "War is hell," she said, laying a hand impulsively on his arm. "It sounds like they were particularly hard in your country. I imagine, with their technology, that wasn't difficult."

Leontios looked down.

"Whatever the Egyptians may have done to your people was returned to them full measure. The British have decided to 'protect' Egypt—in other words, take control of their resources. This is why

Father and I felt safe to visit so soon after the war ended. Looks like the Egyptians are not done fighting. But, Leontios, if you are an enemy of Egypt, what are you doing so far inside its borders?"

"You called me," he said, meeting her eyes and staring deep into her. "You called me, and I am here."

"Of course, it would be that," Violet muttered. "Handsome, foreign man who cannot resist me. What a dream."

"What was that?"

Violet's face burned hotter than the setting desert sun. "Nothing. You're right. We cannot charge the train and hope to rescue anyone. We need help. Reinforcements. I suppose we should enlist some British troops. They won't be happy with today's unrest, but they will be interested in removing my father from the hands of the Egyptian nationalists."

"Where do we go?" he asked.

"I'm not sure," Violet replied. "There are British troops in Alexandria, of course. If we go back to the way the train came, we should easily find help. But we could also go on. Go to the capital in Cairo."

"This to you is completing the journey you set out on," Leontios guessed.

"I suppose. It may be silly, but I do want to see Cairo, even if my entire vacation is ruined. To be honest, it may be closer to where we are now. I'm not sure how long I spent... um, busy while the train was running. You're from this area. Do you know where we are?"

Leontios shook his head. "Nothing here looks familiar to me."

"I suppose we find a way to sneak past the Egyptian nationals and follow the tracks to Cairo then," Violet proposed. "It's the only way I can think of to get help for my father and the others, and honestly, I don't feel safe here in the open."

"We may be safer here," he pointed out. "At least until nightfall. We can move more freely at night."

"We." Violet closed her eyes, still more than half convinced she was dreaming, despite how her calf throbbed. "Well, if I'm unconscious and hallucinating, I might as well enjoy it. What do you suggest, high priest?"

Leontios's eyebrows lifted, but he refrained from commenting. "What I suggested. We wait here until nightfall and then take your suggestion. Follow the... tracks? The tracks to the city of your choosing and enlist the aid of the enemies of our enemies. How far a walk do you think it will be?"

Violet shrugged. "Hard to say. I really wasn't paying attention to time. I was... reading a book."

"The quest for knowledge is as important to the

soul as the search for water is to the body," he said solemnly. It sounded like a quote.

"I've always enjoyed it," she agreed, rolling onto her back and closing her eyes. "How are we supposed to wait until nightfall *or* move on without water? It's hot as blazes even now at sunset."

"Do you have a vessel?" he asked.

Violet opened her eyes and tugged her handbag up to her chest. In the conversation, she'd almost forgotten it. "Let's see. I have a few dollars and some Egyptian money… a crystal… a ceramic disc…my derringer and… Aha!"

She pulled out a metal flask. A thimbleful of liquid sloshed in the bottom. "Actually, this is good." She screwed off the top, gritted her teeth and lifted the corner of her skirt, baring her scrape. Drawing in a hissing breath between her teeth, she upended the brandy onto her injury and then whimpered as quietly as she could manage as the liquor stung her. "There. Couldn't drink it anyway and risk more dehydration, but at least it served a purpose. Father will be unhappy he asked me to carry it." She snickered. "There. A vessel. What do you plan to do with it? Conjure water out of the air?"

"Actually, yes," Leontios replied. "Exactly that."

Violet shook her head. *This is by far the strangest dream I have ever had. I wonder if I will remember it when I wake up.*

Leontios made a movement with his hands, drawing Violet's attention. He reached out toward the setting sun. A beam of light shot directly onto his face, casting his chiseled, tattooed features in shadow. His beard gleamed. His dark eyes flashed. He closed his hands into fists. The beam of light shattered into sparkles. Extending two fingers, Leontios stirred the air. Stirred the sparkles.

"The vessel," he ordered.

Lowering her eyebrows in confusion, Violet lifted the empty flask.

Another movement. The twinkling lights swirled around and around, creating a dark, in-verted cone of a vortex in the middle. From this darkened space, a drop fell into the flask, then an-other and another until a thin stream of water filled the container to the brim.

Leontios released his closed fists, and the sparks winked out.

"Magic?" Violet asked, glad she was sitting so her shaking knees wouldn't drop her onto the sand, spilling the precious beverage.

He smiled.

CHAPTER 6

"Are you sure no one is following us?" Violet asked, peeking over her shoulder for a glimpse of moonlight reflecting off rifles or machine guns. She saw nothing but the long stretch of train tracks.

"I do not detect anyone," Leontios replied, shuffling his soft leather boots in the sand. "Though my powers are not nearly as strong by moonlight."

"Powers," Violet said, shivering. With the sun gone, the desert had become uncomfortably chilly. She wished for the shawl stowed away in her luggage.

"Yes, VioletWarren. Surely you have noticed. Our worlds are very different, but I did pull water out of the desert air."

"Eventually I will wake up," she muttered.

"You are not dreaming," Leontios said. "Has this world no magic then?"

"Very little," Violet admitted. "I've been searching for it since I was a child. My grandmother used to tell me stories of fairies and pirates and little boys who never grew up. I wanted to find my own legend, but so far, I've found more charlatans than true sorcerers. You'll forgive me if I remain skeptical, though the water trick was intriguing."

Leontios stopped walking and turned to face her. "Without magic, how do you live?"

"I don't know," Violet replied. She shuffled on, trying to avoid getting sand into her boots. "Life seems normal to me. What do you mean by live? What do you use magic for... apart from finding water in the desert?"

"Water is a good start. It is scarce. How do you live without it?"

"Water is plentiful where I live," she replied. "It's far from the desert."

"Plentiful...*water?*" Leontios stared.

"You didn't get out of your country much, did you?" Violet asked, her voice kind.

He shook his head. "Travel is difficult, and I was needed at home. I did go to Memphis once, when I was a child, before Egypt turned on us."

"That sounds interesting," Violet said. "Another lover of antiquities, eh?"

He squinted. "There was a religious ceremony.

Our faiths are… not the same, but we do have some gods in common."

"Hmmm," Violet said. *Did he say God or gods? Perhaps his people are a different branch of Islam. I hear there are many but aren't they all monotheistic? Isn't that one of the founding tenets?* She couldn't puzzle it out. As to why he had the same name she had discovered on the cover of her book, she didn't try to explain. *Maybe the name isn't there. Maybe the whole incident of reading the book took place after I hit my head.* That this also did not make sense did dawn on her, but she pushed it away. *A flaw in my memory of the timeline, at least, is rational. More rational than having a stranger whose name happens to match a name written on my book appear in my train at the moment we were attacked by Egyptian freedom fighters and that I'm now walking with along the train tracks to Cairo, in the dark, having a conversation as though we'd been formally introduced and were chatting idly at a party filled with onlookers.*

They walked on in silence; Violet lost in confused ruminations. Leontios seemed to be scanning the horizon with intense scrutiny.

"Do you see anything you recognize?" Violet asked softly.

Leontios shook his head. "I do not think I have ever been in this place. If there is no magic in your world, VioletWarren, how did you summon me?"

"I have no idea," she admitted. "It wasn't intentional."

He glanced at her.

"No offense. I had no idea summoning was an option."

He nodded. "It is unwise to play with spell books, you know."

"So I've learned. Of course, you have to admit that if magic doesn't exist, a spell book is nothing more than a curiosity. I also can't read your language, so I didn't realize the book I've been carrying around for years *was* a spell book."

"What other kinds of books are there?" he demanded, turning to face Violet with a thunderstruck expression.

"Many," she replied. "Works of history, fiction stories, books about mathematics and science and…. I've lost you, haven't I?"

Leontios pursed his lips.

Violet couldn't help but notice how the movement highlighted his tidy beard and etched grooves around his mouth. It suited him.

This dream grows more disturbing by the hour. The handsomest man I've ever met, comfortably chatting with me in the moonlight, making no move to take advantage, listening to my opinion… Why couldn't something like this happen in real life? "Um, are you well?" she asked him, forcing herself out of her rumination and back to the present. *On the off chance that I'm not in a coma right now, I need to stay alert. I am alone in the desert in a foreign country with a total stranger at night.*

"I am trying to understand how leaders are selected when you have no mages," he explained. "It is true, is it not? If there is little concept of magic, mages are not part of your daily life?"

"There are different ways," she replied, diving back into casual conversation. "Some countries have inherited monarchies, though they're growing increasingly rare and depleted of power. Many countries are opting for elections…"

Somehow, his puzzled look didn't surprise her.

"Elections are when the people select their leader."

The look of disgust on Leontios's face spoke volumes.

"I take it you don't approve?"

"What do farmers know of leadership?" he demanded.

Violet shrugged. "It makes sense to me. My country is one of the forerunners of letting the people choose their leader. It's been our way since long before my parents were born. How do your people select leaders? Does the mage make the choice?"

"Nothing like that," he replied. "I think your idea of inherited leadership holds truest. Of course, the son of the prince will be prince. Our confirmation comes when the brother of the prince shows affinity to the sun, as I did. At times, the gods have withdrawn their favor from a family. The presence of a male mage in the family is a sign of the gods' favor. The oldest brother of the mage is the prince. That is the way it has always been for my people."

Violet had to bite her tongue to prevent herself from blurting out how primitive that sounded. Unsure what to say next, she fell into silence, examining the moonlight glinting off the endless miles of train track. *We have a long way to go. I wonder how long. I really wasn't paying attention. Back to Alexandria might have been a better choice. Or maybe not. Was I busy studying for an hour? For two? I didn't make much progress since it was so challenging. Would Father have stayed in the dining car for two hours? He might. When he can be dragged out in public, he's always been gregarious, despite his grumpy protestations.*

Father. What's become of you? What will become of us?

"You are thinking very deeply, VioletWarren," Leontios pointed out.

"I'm worried about my father," she admitted, "and also about us. There are many miles between the cities. I don't know how long I was absorbed in my book. The way back might be shorter than the way ahead, or it might be longer. I really don't know. The only thing I know is that if we follow the train tracks, we'll get there eventually."

"Then that is what we must do. Your instincts urged you to move forward, not back. That will lead us to certain help. If it takes some days, we will persevere."

"Why do you trust me?" she demanded. "I'm a total stranger to you. I might be leading you to your doom for all you know."

Leontios smiled. It looked a little smug. "You called me, Violet. You summoned me from my long sleep. You would not have been able to do this if your intentions were evil. No friend of my enemies could have summoned me."

"But I didn't mean to summon you," she reminded him. "I don't even exactly know what that means. Maybe if I'd had time to read more of what was in your book… it was your book, wasn't it?"

Leontios smirked again. "Yes, surely. That is how you summoned me. You called me by my name, heart open and intention pure. You spoke the incantation of the sun and moon. If you had read more of my book, you would have learned much about such things."

"Sadly, that chance is lost."

He showed her confused eyebrows.

"I didn't find it. We left the train in a hurry, as you might recall."

"Never mind about that," Leontios urged. "I know all that is there. I am happy to share."

"I appreciate the offer," Violet said sadly. "However, the book was *mine.* My constant companion for many years. Its secrets were not all I cared about. I will miss it long before you go back to wherever you came from."

Leontios grabbed Violet's arm, turning her toward him. He looked deep into her eyes, his expression considering. "There is much you do not understand, VioletWarren," he said solemnly.

"Then we have that in common," she shot back.

"Indeed. May I ask you a question?"

"You have been steadily along. Is this question different?"

He didn't address her quip. "Does the moon make you feel more alive?"

This was so far from the line of thought Violet had been expecting, she nearly choked on it. Unsure what to say, she stepped forward several paces, her unexpected companion trotting beside her. "I have no idea," she said at last. "My opportunities to be out in moonlight without someone chattering at me have been limited. Why do you ask?"

"You have been restricted from the moon? Why?"

"It's not safe, of course," she said. "As a woman —a young-ish and, if I dare say, a rather attractive woman—being alone at night, even just to admire the moon, is not advised."

Again, Leontios appeared thunderstruck. "What is not safe?"

"Being out at night alone. Leontios, what kind of society do you live in that you don't know this? I would hate to think you're one of those types of men who doesn't believe other people's problems exist, just because he can't see them." *But* why *would you hate that?* she asked herself. *You don't know this man. He's not even from your culture or anything remotely similar. You can scarcely expect to mean anything more to each other than this passing moment of assistance.*

"It is my duty," he told her solemnly, "to be aware of other people's problems. My role as priest is not merely to commune with the gods. I must also provide spiritual leadership to my people, whether they ask for it or not. I must be aware of undercurrents, issues, fears. Anything that prevents people from being happy and productive." He paused.

Another thought occurred to Violet. "Do your women have to stay indoors then? I've heard that rule applies in some places. They may not leave the family compound without permission, and when they do leave, they must be heavily covered. Is that it?"

He shook his head. "Nothing like that. Violet-Warren, what do you fear will happen late at night?"

"Rape, for one," she told him bluntly. "Men who find women out alone at night often feel they are available, whether the woman in question agrees or not. There's also a great deal of concern about women's chastity. That if they're unsupervised, they might succumb to a seducer and lose their virtue… You look lost again."

"I do not understand much of what you are saying, but I do not think I like your world," he said finally.

Violet opened her mouth to ask more questions when a sound off to their right alerted them both.

They both dropped, hiding behind a convenient clump of bushes.

"What was that?" she whispered, her lips close to her strange companion's ear.

"Could be a jackal," he murmured, "but I do not think so. I think it is a man."

She knew what he meant. For some reason, the freedom fighter they'd seen reprimanded on the train was out there, somewhere, still stalking them. He'd abandoned his group and come after them for reasons of his own. "What should we do?" she whispered.

Leontios made a slashing motion with his hand, urging silence. Moments later, something whizzed over their heads.

"Damn it," Violet whispered, noticing the moonlight flashing on the metallic portions of a distant rifle.

"Does your mysterious bag conceal a weapon?"

"It does," she admitted, reaching inside to stroke a finger over the smooth seashell inlay, "but a poor one. I'd have to be much closer to make use of it, and it only holds two shots. We should save it until we know it won't be wasted."

Leontios's confused look spoke volumes, but he moved on, seeming to trust her judgment. "Whatever it is about us that upset this person," Leontios breathed, "he has not given up. Let us try a more adaptable strategy. Are you sure you cannot channel moon energy?"

"How?" Violet whispered in return. "How will that help?"

"If you can call clouds across the moon, you can conceal us from our enemy. Close your eyes."

Though cutting off one of her senses while an unseen enemy with a weapon fired at them, something about Leontios made her hesitate to argue. She let her lids fall.

"Think of the moon. Feel its light. The soft warmth. The golden glow. Imagine its craggy face. The moon is a woman, like you. Your womb fills and empties as she does. Your feelings rise and fall with hers."

Though the uncouth references made Violet's face flame, the imagery compelled her. She could feel her credulity opening… opening… a golden warmth flooded her.

"The moon is our savior… and our betrayer. Her

light makes us visible, just as she revealed us to our enemy. Call a cloud to cover the light. Call to the elements and bring them to our aid. We wish our enemy no harm. We only wish to escape unnoticed, like a doe in the desert. Do you feel that, VioletWarren?"

"I feel," she breathed.

The quality of darkness changed behind her eyelids. Violet opened her eyes. Clouds had crept across the moon, blocking its light.

"Well done," her companion breathed. "Can you move in silence, Violet?"

"I can try," she replied, eyeing her shoes doubtfully. Though selected for walking in uneven terrain, the boots lacked subtlety... and rubber soles. *Good thing it's sand and not undergrowth.* Then she cursed mentally as her feet crunched softly on the yielding surface.

Crouching low, she followed Leontios several paces away from the train tracks into the wilderness, where bushes obscured the view of their whereabouts. From there, he led her in a zigzagging path from shrub to shrub, always with the obvious aim of concealment, until almost an hour had passed, and they lay breathing slowly behind a low hill.

"Think we lost him?" Violet asked in a whisper.

"I do not know," Leontios replied honestly. "Perhaps it is best we keep moving."

"Are you sure we're moving in the right direction? You said you don't recognize the area. Has that changed?"

"It has not," he replied. "However, I can feel those rails you told me your… train? Yes, the train must follow. I cannot see them in the dark, but they radiate the warmth of the sun."

Violet looked askance, but it was far from the strangest thing she'd experienced thus far. *When I longed for adventure, this isn't what I meant.*

They pressed on again, and slowly it dawned on Violet that she probably wasn't dreaming. *It's been too long. Too much physical sensation. Too much awareness of a sensible passage of time. It's still possible I've been knocked unconscious and that I'm having a very elaborate dream, but this is beginning to seem unlikely. So, where does that lead me?* "Leontios," she whispered.

"Yes, VioletWarren?" he replied in a low rumble that sent tingles up her spine.

"You're real, aren't you? I'm not having a hallucination?"

"I do not know what that means," he replied, "though I can guess it is some kind of unwanted vision. Yes, I am real, though I recommend you not begin to panic."

"I don't think I will," she replied. "At least, not yet. I'm too busy trying to get away from this crazed gunman and toward help. I might fall apart later. Time will tell."

"A sensible plan," he agreed. "Perhaps we should talk less. If someone is creeping up behind us, it would be easy to follow our whispers."

Violet nodded.

Leontios crept away, low to the ground, his leather boots silent on the sand.

Amazing for a full-grown man—not that he's unusually large, but he's, well, man-sized—to move so quietly. Despite her own smaller, slighter frame, Violent couldn't prevent herself from crunching sand and snapping twigs. Each soft sound drew an internal curse from Violet as she stumbled along.

Only a short time later, they came to the end of any visible cover.

"Damn," Violet breathed, crouching under the last available shrub.

"Indeed," Leontios agreed, falling to the sand beside her. "What shall we do now, VioletWarren?"

"I wish I knew," she whispered. "I feel pretty trapped. If we run and that idiot is behind us, we become easy targets, and I don't see anywhere to hide up ahead. If we stay, he has all the time in the world to creep up on us. We're stuck."

The dim moonlight filtering through the clouds illuminated Leontios's scowl. "I do not like feeling trapped."

Violet rested her forehead on one arm. Fatigue

dragged at her even as fear kept her weary heart pumping. The combination made her nauseous. She felt a gag lingering at the back of her throat.

Something warm came to rest on her back. She glanced over her shoulder.

Leontios's dark eyes bored into hers, concerned and kind.

She smiled wanly at him. "I'm glad to have known you," she murmured, "even if it was for such a short time."

"Do not lose all hope, Violet," he said gently. "We may yet prevail. What is the nature of this weapon?"

"It's a rifle," she said.

His face took on that baffled expression she had already seen so many times.

She opened her mouth to try to explain and then closed it again, not sure how much common ground they had to build on, let alone how to describe something whose internal mechanisms she didn't fully understand.

"Show me," he urged, extending one hand.

Violet gulped. "The last time I 'showed' you something, it hurt a lot," she reminded him.

"That was a whole language," he replied. "One concept should sting no more strongly than a sandfly."

Hesitantly, she laid her hand in his. His warm palm, dampened with a faint slick of sweat, felt like life itself in her. It radiated up her arm, across her breasts and calmed her rapid pulse to a slow, steady thump. Her lungs expanded as sunlit air—in defiance of the moonlight— filled her belly. A tingle flared to life and spread lower, awakening parts of her no one had ever touched. For a moment, she felt alive—truly alive—for the first time.

The sting in her fingertips barely registered over the thrumming heat in her core.

Then, the tantalizing warmth withdrew from her skin. "I see," Leontios whispered. "That is a serious problem. However, it should not be insurmountable. This is not a hail of arrows or an army of spears. It is one man with one projectile. Troublesome but limited."

"How do you mean?" she hissed. "He doesn't have to get close to kill us! I…" what she was going to say next faded away. Violet's eyebrows drew together, and she listened to a strange rumble, an irregular hum coming from the far horizon in the direction they were heading.

"What is it?" Leontios asked.

Without further reflection, Violet stood and ran.

CHAPTER 7

*V*iolet's heart pounded harder than ever. Her breath rasped in her burning chest. The compelling warmth Leontios had generated in her evaporated like dew in the sun, supplanted by burgeoning excitement.

"Help us!" she cried in English.

An explosion sounded behind her, and she dodged to the left.

"Help! Help!"

A shout responded. "Who goes there?"

"Help us!" she screamed and then threw herself flat into the sand.

In the distance, the rifle fired again.

Leontios slammed into Violet's back, covering her with his body. The bullet whizzed over their heads.

"Thanks," she muttered.

"Who are you calling, VioletWarren?" Leontios demanded, ignoring the courtesy, "and how do you know they are a friend?"

"I can hear them. They're speaking English. *British* English. These are the people we're looking for."

"Interesting," Leontios said blandly, hauling Violet to her feet and taking her hand. "I hope you are correct. However, our enemy is drawing closer. We should retreat." He began to run forward, dodging to the right and then to the left, seemingly at random, dragging Violet along with him. Though not overly long-legged, his explosive speed left her stumbling to keep up.

The gun fired again, a projectile whizzing into the space where they had been a moment before, just as a herd of mounted soldiers clattered over a distant hill. The clouds parted, and the moonlight glinted on the light skin and pale hair of Europeans in tan uniforms and domes of helmets.

"Help me!" Violet screamed, dashing straight at the horses.

"Good God!" she heard one of the soldiers exclaimed. The bouncing of the animals rendered the speaker invisible, but his welcome British accent carried through the dry, still air to her ears. "That woman! She needs us."

Leontios yanked Violet to the side as another

bullet exploded through the space she'd just occupied.

"Watch out!" another shout sounded from horseback. "He's got her."

The soldiers drew close and bounced to a stop. Men leaped to the ground and trained weapons at Leontios.

"Stop!" Violet yelled. "Not him. He's with me. Someone is chasing us!"

"Are you saying you're 'with' this Egyptian?" the man closest to her—a blond man with crooked front teeth—demanded.

"I am *not* Egyptian," Leontios snarled.

"No, no," Violet snapped. "Listen, he's fine. He's… he's my father's manservant. He's… Mexican. It can be hard to tell. You need to deal with the Egyptian who's *shooting* at us. I'll explain the rest later."

"As milady wishes." The young man tipped his hat and fired a warning shot. "You there. Begone. You have one chance to disappear or have a taste of lead."

Silence fell. The night itself seemed to be considering its options. Beside her, in a barely audible breath, Leontios murmured words she felt she could almost understand. Almost without thought, Violet reached out to the night again. Clouds closed in, thick and heavy, obscuring the view.

"What's it going to be, friend?" the soldier challenged. "There are a whole lot of us and only one of you. Care to try your luck?"

Footsteps crunched ostentatiously as the unseen threat retreated.

Violet sagged, leaning against Leontios.

"All right, Miss. He's gone. Now, what do you have to say for yourself? What is an American lass doing alone in the Egyptian desert with a 'Mexican' manservant, chased by a rifle-wielding maniac?"

"I know, I know." Violet took a deep breath. "My name is Violet Warren. My father and I… and Leo here, of course, well we were coming to see Cairo. Father is a steel tycoon. We've got a hobby of adventuring around the world's ancient places. With the war over, we decided on Egypt, and…"

"Miss… uh, Miss?" the man interrupted.

Violet trailed off.

"Not commenting on the wisdom of coming to a country that's still experiencing… unrest—not to mention illness—but… what were you doing running through the night alone with… him?" He gestured with his rifle.

"Our train was attacked. Leo helped me escape. We were going to Cairo to get help."

"You were on the train?"

She nodded. "It seemed someone was determined we would not escape." She bit her lip. "Did you know about it?"

"We knew it didn't arrive as scheduled. With all

87

the unrest, it was more likely an attack than a derailment. But what's this, now, Miss? No need to get upset. We'll watch over you. You're safe."

"It's…" Violet's voice wavered, and she leaned harder on Leontios. He gripped her elbow, the warmth of his hand sinking through the sleeve of her blouse and making a tingle run up her arm. "It's my… my father," she stammered. "He didn't get off the train. He's not a young man, and I'm worried about him." She sniffled, a sob choking off her throat.

"There, there." The soldier dug into his pouch and withdrew a handkerchief, extending it to Violet.

She waved away the offer. *Someone else's grippe hankie? Disgusting. I think not.* "I'm all right. I'll cry later. What do we do now?"

"You and your… and this fellow will head on to Cairo, Miss Warren. We'll send a couple of men to protect you from your… friend back there. Thank you for letting us know about the attack. We weren't sure, but now, we'll be prepared."

"And my father?"

"We will bring any survivors to Cairo. I suggest you stay at the Shepheard's Hotel. It will make it easier for us to direct him to you. I will look you up myself when I get back from this… little mission and let you know."

"I appreciate that." Violet extended a hand, and

he took it, eyeing her consideringly, as though wondering whether to shake or kiss. Violet made the decision for him, giving a hard pump and then gently slipping her fingers out of his grasp.

"Ennis, Bilbrey!" the officer shouted, "take Miss Warren to Cairo. Make sure she finds her way to the hotel."

"This way, Miss Warren," a man near the back of the group called.

Violet tried to step forward, but she swayed.

"Be careful, Miss Warren," Leontios said as his gentle grasp on her arm firmed. "You've been through a difficult time. Let me help you." He took more of her weight onto himself and escorted her among the horses.

One whickered near him, and he shied away from it, bringing him a bit too close to another skittish mount, which pawed the earth. He froze.

"Easy," Violet murmured, not wanting to embarrass him. Feeling stronger, she took a step away from Leontios, slipping her hand into his to lead him, threading a path between the antsy horses.

"We don't have any extra mounts, Ma'am," the soldier said sadly. "You can have mine if you think you can handle him, but your man will have to walk."

"I will be fine on foot," Leontios said solemnly, but Violet could feel a faint shudder running through his arm.

"Honestly, I'm not a good rider," Violet said. "I'm not comfortable with these war horses. Do we have far to go?"

"About two miles," the man replied.

She nodded. "I can manage that."

The two men slipped from their saddles. "This way then," the second man, the dark-haired one, said.

The rest of the men began to trot away as Violet, Leontios and their escorts moved off toward the South, where she now knew Cairo lay.

"We must be nearly to the outskirts if it's only a two-mile walk to the hotel," she commented.

"Aye," the dark-haired man grunted.

"Which one are you?" she asked him.

"He's Ennis," the blond replied and then muttered, "Stubborn Scott," under his breath.

Ennis scowled at the teasing.

"You must be Bilbrey," Violet guessed.

"Indeed. Horace Carter Bilbrey the third, at your service." He swept off his hat and bowed. His horse, uncomfortable with the movement, snorted a warning, which drew Leontios to a sudden stop.

"Goodness!" Violet covered the awkward moment with a girlish exclamation. "That's *quite* a powerful name. What's a gentleman like you doing in the army?"

He grinned, setting his hat back on his head. "The name is more powerful than the family, I'm afraid. Not only is my father a most noble butcher, but there are also nine of us. It was the army or sweeping unmentionable bits all day long. At least this way, I get to see the world."

"Ah," Violet replied. She took a step forward, tugging gently on Leontios's hand. He stumbled into motion but soon caught up with a smooth rhythm.

Feeling eyes on her, Violet scanned their companions and found Ennis staring at her, or rather at her hand, where it clutched Leontios's. She let go abruptly.

"Where do you hail from, Miss?" Bilbrey asked.

"Pittsburgh," she replied absently, making idle conversation for no other reason than to pass the time. "Have you ever been to the States?"

"Never have," he replied. "Never felt a need. I had no idea there were such charming ladies there. Perhaps I should rethink my stance."

Violet blushed at the compliment. It occurred to her how young the flirtatious soldier was, probably almost a decade younger than her, and her blush deepened.

"What brought you all the way to Egypt?" Bilbrey continued. "Was it, like you said, just a vacation?"

"Exactly," Violet replied.

"Taking a vacation into the heart of civil unrest and illness is not perhaps the wisest decision." His voice took on a condescending tone as though talking to a child.

Violet's teeth clenched.

"Civil unrest?" Leontios asked. "Seems to me more like an invasion. Your people clearly are not from here. Are you conquerors?" Beneath the bland surface of the question, Violet could almost hear the gears turning in Leontios's mind.

"What do you care?" Ennis snapped.

"The young lady is in my care," Leontios replied. "I take her safety seriously. Freedom fighters, those looking to free their land from hostile invaders, are hard to stop."

"They're nothing but a desert rabble," Bilbrey said, his light tone hardening. "They'll not stand a chance."

"Damned Egyptians don't know what's best for themselves," Ennis muttered. "They don't realize how much we want to help them."

"To answer your question, Leo," Violet said brightly, almost chirping like a bird, "the British are *great* conquerors. They have left the stamp of their empire in *so many places*. This is one of them. The saying goes, the sun never sets on the British empire." She glanced at Leontios and saw that once again he lacked the context to understand the comment, so she turned to Ennis and Bilbrey. "Gentlemen, don't forget how vast the ocean is. I didn't hear about the unrest and had hoped the British presence in Egypt would make our vacation safer. I also heard the grippe was waning in this part of the world. I suppose I misunderstood. I do hope we can recover my father and that he's unharmed." Her voice wavered. Though not entirely feigned, she exaggerated the reaction, leading the men into comfortable thought territory. Somehow it seemed very important for them not to realize too much about her.

As the first structures on the outskirts of Cairo appeared on the horizon, Violet fell into a comfortable pattern of light conversation with Bilbrey, distracting him with a featherhead routine she'd long since perfected at her father's many social obligations. It embarrassed her a little to put on such an act in front of Leontios, but it kept Bilbrey occupied and prevented probing questions she didn't know how to answer.

As the sun began to glow behind the buildings of Cairo, they arrived at their destination. A four-story tan structure with a flat front and the name, Shepheard's Hotel, posted over the roof in a wire frame.

"Will you be able to afford a room for a few days, ma'am?" Bilbrey asked. "I don't have much myself, but I can ask around."

"I can manage," Violet assured him, thinking of the banknotes in her handbag. "Thank you, sir. I appreciate your help. This is where your people will bring my father?"

"If he's alive," Ennis said.

Violet's voice failed at last. With a nod to Bilbrey, she grabbed Leontios's elbow and walked unsteadily up the stairs and into the hotel.

CHAPTER 8

A delicious aroma wafted up from the white-skirted table. Violet's stomach rumbled. She dipped her spoon in the soup and took a sip. Mutton and vegetables with a heavy dose of spice danced on her tongue.

She tore off a chunk of bread with her teeth and immediately regretted it. Her stomach clenched.

"It's a bit early for soup, isn't it?" Bilbrey, now dressed in a pair of trousers and a plain white shirt instead of a uniform, dropped into a seat across from Violet.

She frowned. In the light of day, he looked even younger than before. "I wanted something simple," she said. "I had a rough day yesterday, remember? I still feel strange."

"No wonder," Bilbrey replied. "Are you

holding up well enough under the circumstances? Far from home with no support, you must be just terrified."

Violet's frown deepened. While he wasn't wrong, something pointed in his expression told her his offer was not all it seemed. She tutted. "I will be fine. Especially when your men bring my father and hopefully my luggage here. I'm quite a seasoned traveler. I have everything I need. It's just that it's on the train. I have nothing to do but wait… and try to eat some food and rest." She pondered whether there was anything else she wanted to say but realized that keeping the conversation going with this silly young man didn't appeal, so she took another bite of bread. This one stayed down just fine, so she chased it with a few more hearty bites of soup.

On a hunch, she squinted her eyes slightly, allowing her crow's feet to show.

Bilbrey's eyes widened. "Well, if you're quite sure you're all right, let me know if you need… anything. I'll see you later." He jumped to his feet and fled.

Violet grinned into her bowl. Then her amusement faded as she recalled just how much bravado she required to cover her upset.

Movement in her peripheral vision drew Violet's attention. She sighed, eyes closing in disgust at having to fend off Bilbrey's advances again. *He's probably decided I'm desperate for 'comforting' and can overcome his revulsion at my agedness.*

"Are you well, VioletWarren?"

Violet's eyes flew open. Leontios sat before her.

"Please just call me Violet, Leontios," she said tiredly. "And to answer your question, no. I am not well at all. Remember, in the past twelve hours, I've been caught up in the attack on a train, been separated from my elderly father, marched through the desert, and been shot at multiple times. I'm too restless to sleep, so I thought eating would be a good idea, but it's not going well either."

He reached across the table and took hold of her hand.

She met his eyes. The warmth and kindness she saw there stole her breath and brought long-suppressed sobs to the surface until they nearly broke through her restraint.

"You have been very strong. You do not need to be ashamed of finally having a reaction."

Violet nodded. "Where have you been?" she asked, changing the subject. "If they sent you to the servants' quarters, I apologize. It was the only explanation I could come up with at the moment."

Leontios shrugged. "I suppose it is a servant's quarters, as you say. There are many beds. The one they gave me is comfortable, if tall. I can only imagine what creeps beneath it. What do you have there?"

"Just a simple soup. Shall I order one for you?"

"That would be much appreciated. There are many things I do not understand about your world. Procuring food is one of those things."

Violet waved to the waiter, and a few minutes later, a second meal arrived. Leontios observed Violet closely and, with an awkward fumble, began to spoon vegetables and broth into his mouth. "Tasty," he said.

"What have you been doing?" she asked.

"I did nothing," he replied. "I sat on the bed for a time and then came looking for you. I was not sure what else was appropriate to do. Remember that this is not my land."

"Nor mine," Violet agreed. "I'm far from home. I hope not to commit any faux pas, but the odds are against me. In my favor, I can apologize in Arabic if I need to."

Leontios raised an eyebrow.

"I don't understand how you can live next to the Egyptians, even be invaded by them, and still know so little about them that you don't even speak or *know about* their language."

"Soon, VioletWar…Violet, you will have to accept some uncomfortable realities about me."

She closed her eyes and took a sip of soup.

"Or do you still believe you are suffering from a head injury?"

She shook her head. "That belief is no longer entirely… believable. I realize you and I need to talk about who you are and why you're here."

He opened his mouth, but she rushed on.

"I know you're Leontios, brother to the Prince of Skeon, high priest of the sun, and you're here because I called you. Honestly, I have no idea what any of that means."

"This will take time… and strain your credulity. Are you certain you want to begin this conversation now?"

"Why not?" Violet took a bite of her bread. "I have nothing else to do until our esteemed friends come back from their mission to retake the train."

"Oh." Leontios turned his attention to his lunch. His intense eyes skated away.

"What does that 'oh' mean?" Violet asked. "There's something more to it, I think."

"I saw you talking to that young warrior. I thought you might prefer to spend more time with him."

"Oh, dear Lord." Violet rolled her eyes. "Leontios, he's much too young for me. Too foolish as well."

Leontios smiled. "Some women are attracted to young fools."

"Some men count on it," Violet snapped back, "including my father. I, however, am not of that sort."

"I am glad to hear it, VioletWarren.... Violet. Or should I say Miss Warren?"

"That would be the most correct address, yes," she agreed. "How on earth did you come up with that?"

"I observed the warriors. Since, as we have both said, we are foreign here, I make note of many things. One was how you were addressed. Explain, please, what Miss means, what Violet and Warren are."

Violet smiled. "Violet is my personal name. Warren is my family name, similar to how you reference your brother in your title. Didn't I explain this before?"

Leontios nodded. "I can better take in the explanation in this safe, quiet place."

Seeing him leaning forward with obvious interest on his face, Violet continued. "Miss is a term of description. It means I am an unmarried woman. Mister would refer to a man and missus for a married woman."

"Ah. Why do your people differentiate women on the presence of a spouse and not men?"

Violet pondered as she took a sip of wine. "You know, I don't know. It's just the way it's done."

"Tradition," he agreed. "Sometimes, after much time has passed, the meaning can be lost."

"I take it then that, in your country, neither a

woman's address nor a man's indicate whether the person is married?"

"No, naturally not. Only a small number of people marry. It is a practice reserved only for the most important members of society. Commoners do not marry."

Violet lowered her eyebrows. "You must not be Muslim then."

"I do not know what that means."

Violet inhaled sharply and sucked a crumb of bread down her throat. She began coughing. In hopes of washing away the offending morsel, she grabbed her glass and sipped, forgetting it contained wine. The sharp sting in her throat only made her cough more.

"Miss?" an unfamiliar voice in Arabic-accented English said at her elbow.

She turned and blinked through streaming eyes at a young waiter who extended a glass of water. She grabbed it unceremoniously and gulped it down.

"Thank you," she rasped.

The man nodded and stepped away. Violet's eyes tracked him.

"I take it," Leontios said dryly, "that you did not expect this statement."

"I did not," Violet replied, her voice hoarse and her eyes still watering. "What on earth can it mean that you lived next to Egypt, and not only do you not recognize their language, but their primary religion is totally foreign to you? But you said you used to worship with them. Explain."

"I can only assume that Egypt has vastly changed. You say this is the capital?"

Violet jerked her chin downward in a curt nod.

"And that these people are Egyptians?"

"Of course they are. Why do you ask such questions?"

"Because I do not recognize them. They do not look like Egyptians, sound like them or dress like them. What you say about their language and religion does not resemble anything I know about our enemies. They were once our friends, and I knew their language and customs well. Our religions shared many common points. This can only mean that much time has passed while I was insensible."

"Insensible?"

"Violet, you are intelligent, but you fear the truth. Perhaps our escape in the night proved too distracting for you to *think*. Did it occur to you to wonder where your book went, why you could not find it when you exited the… the train? Why you called the name on the book and invoked the spell while intending to know me, and I appeared?"

"Are you going to say it's magic?" she demanded darkly.

"Of course. You summoned me using the spells in my spell book."

Violet squinted at Leontios. "I called you by reading the book? Where were you then?"

"Violet," he said, his voice soft and intense, "I *am* the book."

Violet spooned soup into her mouth and swallowed without tasting it. No thoughts crowded through her normally busy mind. Nothing coherent anyway. Physical sensations raged. Her face felt hot. A strange buzzing noise sounded in her ears. Her belly bounced up and down as though she had boarded a ship. But actual word-type thoughts ceased to exist. Long moments drew out while she stared into her bowl, examining each snippet of food as it floated up in the broth.

"Will you say nothing then?" Leontios asked at length.

"Nothing," Violet agreed. "What on earth could I say to something like that? Eat your soup."

Mercifully, he did.

With every bite, the words—the bomb he had just lobbed into the conversation—tried to bubble up. It required no effort for her to push it away. A plate of mental steel had slammed shut, and the strange words bounced off it over and over, but each reverberation rebounded with the impact of a gong.

By the time she had finished her meal, the constant beating of Leontios's words against her awareness had drained away the last of her nervous energy. "I'm going to lie down," she said woodenly. "Maybe you should do the same."

Without another word, without a backward glance, she stalked to the stairs and climbed. With every floor, the heat increased until sweat beaded on her forehead, but she paid it no mind. She felt numb, so numb she wondered if she would ever feel anything again, as though the last shock had not just shaken her. It had killed off something in her soul. She stumbled into her stuffy room and collapsed onto her bed. Her clumsy fingers fumbled with the laces of her boots, but at last, she dragged them from her feet. She flopped onto the pillow. Unconsciousness dragged her under in an instant.

Of course, Violet's busy mind didn't stop just because her body had given up. In her sleep, she dreamed. Strange dreams of a time and place she did not understand, yet in her dream, nothing seemed foreign. It felt like home in a way that nothing had in her whole life. And when she woke, a dreamy sense of calm and peace had descended on her. While her conscious mind worried about her father, something deeper than thought, deeper than awareness, seemed to bubble up from deep within.

Rising from the bed, she stretched, spared a

single glance for the hot, plain room in which she'd agreed to stay pending the arrival of the army and the captives, and turned to a small stand at the foot of the bed. There, she found, as expected, a pitcher of tepid water, which she poured into a large porcelain bowl, splashing some on her face and neck. Though the water washed away some of the sweaty sensations from her nap, it did nothing to break through her lethargy. She tugged on her boots, leaving the laces dangling.

Floating rather than walking, she made her way out of the hotel room, locked the door without much attention and dropped the key into her bag. Though still not connecting to coherent thoughts, she made her way back down the stairs, past the hotel restaurant and out into the street. She had no particular destination in mind, but her feet, it seemed, had a plan of their own. They led her away from the hotel into the densely packed streets with confidence unwarranted in a woman who had never been there before and had only studied a few maps. She covered ground quickly, ignoring the hawkers that lined the streets, offering everything from 'genuine' Egyptian papyrus made of banana leaves painted in the last hour to fabulous gold and silver jewelry to loose robes of cotton in vibrant colors until she found herself in a small souk, redolent with spices, where puffs of tobacco smoke floated out of one shop. She stopped moving and turned in a slow circle, wondering where she had ended up.

"Where are we going, VioletWarren?"

In her state of extreme relaxation, Violet felt only mild surprise at Leontios's unexpected appearance. "I'm not sure," she replied. "I knew there was a market near the hotel. It was on the list of things I wanted to do while here."

"VioletWarren… Violet. What has happened to you? You cannot wander through unknown streets in the heat of the day. The sun is very strong, and the air is too hot."

Violet blinked, finally noticing the sweat beading on her forehead.

"You know—you knew yesterday—that the heat is too much for you."

Violet ignored him. She ignored the crowd in the street, though they pressed in on all sides, robes brushing her from all directions. She felt like something was calling her from a distance. A long way off in the desert, something from the dream—which she could barely remember—wanted her to come to it.

"VioletWarren, we must return to the… the hotel. Now. You cannot wander this way. If you become lost, I will not be able to help you. I do not know this place either. Please come now." Leontios took her arm and turned her away from the compelling scene.

Egypt. Real, vital Egypt pulsed like a heartbeat *here*. It reminded her of her dream, the dream she couldn't quite remember. *There were ancient things there, as there are here. And it's alive. So much has changed. So much was lost. If only real ancient Egyptians still walked these streets. I think they would like to smoke. They were a bawdy lot.*

His grip on her arm, though gentle, remained unbreakable as he led her away from where she wanted to go—much deeper into the souk, into the mysteries of what her beloved Egypt had become.

"I need… I want…"

"You are acting strangely," he informed her solemnly. "I think you are not fully awake. Perhaps you should return to your room and sleep more."

"You've known me less than a day," Violet groused, grumpy at being thwarted. "How do you know if I'm acting strangely."

Leontios paused and turned to look down into her face. Somehow, the same energy from whatever it was out in the desert burned in his eyes.

Such lovely eyes. Though warm and dark, they also burn with an unfamiliar fire. This is not a man who loves money. His passion is for something deeper. It rings in harmony with me. Violet pursed her lips slightly, only partially conscious of what she was doing, what she was asking for. *Here, I can still feel the beating heart of my beloved Egypt. Of the ancient. It beats in Leontios. Could he really be what he said? I can almost believe it.*

"I know you, VioletWarren. You called me, remember? I took your language right from your hand. I know more than you realize. We are connected, you and I. That is how I knew you left the hotel. I can feel you drawing away from me. And that is how I know that you, who knew so much about moving safely through the desert yesterday, suddenly look like a bewildered child."

Violet closed her eyes, not taking in his meaning at all. She felt as caught in his presence as she did in the living presence of Egypt itself. His voice and gaze had as much intensity as a kiss, but he hadn't taken the invitation. *And why am I inviting him anyway? He appeared out of nowhere yesterday. He claims to be a book. He's mad, or at least very strange… strange and compelling.* Without meaning to, her fingers lifted to trace the tattoo at his temple. "What does it mean?" she asked.

"It is an invocation to our god, the sun," he replied off-handedly. "Please, Violet, we must return to the hotel now. If you wish to explore, we should do so when the sun is lower and the heat breaks." He took hold of her hand and turned back, determinedly walking back the way they had come. This time, Violet followed his lead, docile as a lamb.

He is so much more than just a man. Surely, he is not crazy but… different. Some other thing I cannot fully place… or understand. He is everything I have wished for. Everything I desire. If only he really could be my book brought to life and teach me all the secrets I spent so many years pondering.

Leontios led Violet back to the hotel and through the door into the dining room where she had eaten soup hours earlier.

"Excuse me," he said, waving to a hurrying waiter. The young man approached. "This young woman is a guest at your establishment, and she has suffered a shock. Do you have anything bracing that can help her?"

"Tea?" the waiter suggested. "I can make it extra sweet to wake her up."

Leontios looked deep into Violet's eyes. "Do you want tea, Miss Warren?"

"Tea… sounds good," Violet conceded. She didn't notice the waiter leave because her attention was entirely focused on Leontios. On his lovely dark eyes, his tidy black beard. The tattoos at his temples and on his neck. "I dreamed about you," she breathed. "I forgot until now, but you were with me when I slept."

He nodded. "Not surprising. What did you dream?"

She shook her head. "It was so strange. I dreamed I was in the desert, in a city of moss and vines. There was something there. A huge crystal. It hummed and… and it called to me."

"That is good."

The waiter returned in a flurry of indistinct peripheral movement she felt no urge to consider as she chattered on. "And the moon hung so big and low in the sky. I felt like it was calling me too. I wanted to answer, but I didn't know the words. Then you appeared. You told me the words I needed and…" she trailed off, realizing she didn't want to reveal the rest of her dream in all its enticing explicitness. *Not that. How would I even explain without looking like a hussy?* She looked up into the shining obsidian of Leontios's eyes. "What does it mean?"

One side of his mouth lifted in a half-grin. "You will know when the time is right, I am sure. For now, you should drink your tea. Here it is." He handed her a cup.

Violet looked at the cup. In her dreamy state, its flowered pattern seemed to float in front of her eyes. It took her three tries to grasp the delicate porcelain. However, at the first sip of the hot, sugared beverage, Violet snapped with a start out of her lethargy. She blinked several times. "What's happening?"

"You were behaving strangely when you awoke. Do you not remember wandering in the street? I have brought you back to the hotel and procured you a drink. VioletWarren, what is tea?"

"Try some," she suggested, extending the cup.

He took a sip, grimaced and handed it back. Then he rose from his knees and sat in a chair beside her.

"Thank you for bringing me back. I can't imagine what possessed me." She wiped sweat off her forehead, surprised by her own uncharacteristically careless behavior. *What on earth was I thinking, wandering alone into the streets in the heat of the day with no map? And it is so hot. So much hotter than I would have expected. I must have lost my mind.* Embarrassed, she decided to change the subject quickly.

"So, I must admit I'm puzzled," she said, "about this place where you live. Since there's nothing to do but wait until we hear… hear that my father is all right, and since it's too hot to go out into the sun —it's hotter than I expected for so early in the year. It must be over eighty degrees—we have time to talk. I've asked before, but now I'd like you to explain. How is it that you say your land was overtaken by the Egyptians, but you don't know anything about Egypt? You don't recognize the religion, the language or the people. You talk about the Egypt I read about in ancient papyri. It's as though you are describing the Egypt of long ago." She didn't bring up the claim of him being a book. Her mind rejected such nonsense, of course, but she couldn't understand how to reconcile such nonsense with such a stern and serious soul. He didn't seem crazy.

"I can only imagine," he replied, "as I have said, that many years have passed while I was insensible."

"Well, perhaps. If you were injured in the war and in a coma, it might last a number of weeks. People who remain unconscious for longer than that rarely wake up, and if they do, they're never quite the same again. But, Leontios, that still doesn't make sense. The Egypt you describe has been, well, extinct for a very long time."

"How long?" His eyes grew even more intense. He leaned forward, probing as though this were not the idlest of conversations. His hand came to rest on hers.

"Hard to say. What was happening in Egypt the last you remember?"

Leontios's compelling dark eyes softened, so he looked far away. "As I have said, once, they were our friends. Though Egypt was larger, we had better magic, so we respected each other. I may have mentioned we had several gods in common, though we worshipped them in different ways. I recall traveling with my father and brother to the capital, to Memphis, to see a massive building project."

Violet gulped. "Was it a pyramid?"

He nodded. "How did you know?"

Violet sank back in her chair because all her

muscles had let loose. Her breath whooshed from her mouth in an inelegant flapping of her lips.

"What is it, VioletWarren?"

"You are describing the rise of Egypt's Old Kingdom," she explained with a tongue that felt almost too lax to move. "It has been over four thousand years since the Great Pyramid was built."

Leontios's face went pale. "Four *thousand* years? By the sun and moon! No wonder I have felt so lost. Everything has changed. Everything. There is nothing left of the world I have known." He sucked in a ragged breath and thumped his chest with his open palm as though to start a faltering heart.

"Nothing except the pyramid itself. It's not far from here, actually."

Leontios did not respond to her inane comment. He gasped, hunched over his belly, one hand braced on the table, the other clutching his chest. He looked as though a giant had dealt him a fatal blow.

And why not, Violet realized, letting the moment take its time. *It's unbelievable.* She tried to grasp it, tried to imagine how she would react to a world in which no person, no place, no concept remained. She failed.

At length, Leontios exhaled heavily. Then he reached out and grabbed Violet's tea, gulping down a generous swig and shuddering at the sugar.

"We have a serious problem, Violet," he said at last.

"What is that?"

Leontios inhaled deeply and released a tea-scented breath that blew the hair back from her face. "I will tell you. I must. I hope you will try to believe me. I realize you already doubt my truthfulness regarding what I have told you. If my story thus far strains your credulity, I can only imagine what the rest of the tale will do to you. However, I swear to you, by all the gods in heaven and on earth, that everything I say is true."

Violet looked deep into his earnest brown eyes, and though her mind longed to reject the utter nonsense he was spewing, her heart trusted him. "Tell me."

"The dream you told me about, with the crystal?"

She nodded.

"It is real. It is the chief relic and most important treasure of Skeon."

Violet looked at him.

"And it is extremely volatile. It collects power from the sun and the moon. One of my chief tasks as high priest of the sun is—along with the high priestess of the moon—to drain the excess power from the crystal and disperse it into the spring that waters our land. I fear that if the power has been building for so many centuries, it may rupture."

"And that would be bad?" Violet asked, eyes wide.

"It would likely destroy everything in the vicinity. Including this hotel and the train and... I do not know how far. But it would be devastating. I am astonished that it has held this long."

"Maybe it will hold indefinitely, then?"

Leontios's throat worked as he considered. "Perhaps, but I dare not simply leave it to chance. Caring for the crystal is my solemn duty. Whether it could hold another day, a hundred years or forever, I must determine for myself. I cannot leave it and assume all will be well."

Violet gulped. "Are you sure it's still there? Ancient treasures have been plundered, well, since ancient times, and waves of invaders, including the French, the Italians and the British, have taken away piles of artifacts. A giant crystal like the one I saw in my dream would likely have been cut up and carried off in antiquity."

"There were many words I did not understand," Leontios said, "but if you are suggesting that the wealth of Skeon has gone the way of the wealth of Egypt—into the hands of foreigners—that could not have happened. For one, Skeon is very small. For another, it is hidden. My last act of magic before we were overrun by Egyptian invaders was to blast them with the full force of the sun's power. The city of Skeon was obliterated, and only the inner court remained, with not one soul who knew its location left alive. The wall itself looks like an ordinary rock within a natural formation in the desert. Without the key, it will be invisible."

Violet sighed. "Invisible and with a bomb inside, pressure building and waiting to erupt."

"I do not understand—"

"Bomb?" Violet guessed. At his nod, she reached out her hand. "I'll visualize one. You can see it if I think it hard enough, right?"

For the first time, Leontios hesitated, but in the end, he consented to touch.

Violet concentrated on the memory of a demonstration she'd once seen of a small hand grenade and the resulting explosion. The throwing up of dust and debris. How the cow carcass on which it had lain had flown to pieces. The sting in her palm told her Leontios had taken the knowledge.

He released her. "The idea is right, but the scope is too small."

"As you mentioned earlier," she reminded him. "But the idea of an explosion?"

He nodded. "Very like that."

Violet drew in a deep breath. "Can you still fix it?"

"If I can find it, I can try. There are many problems with this plan, however."

"Such as?"

"Well, if, as you say, we are near King Djoser's

pyramid, it is many hours' walk to the ruins of Skeon. I do not know what of the landscape has changed. It may all be city. It may all be desert or some combination. I will likely not recognize any landmarks. I also do not have the key, so despite my close connection with the crystal, I might not be able to find it. Finally, the draining of the crystal is done with a moon priestess and a sun priest working together. It cannot be done alone."

Violet frowned. "That sounds daunting. Might it not be better to run away? Put as much distance as possible between us and the crystal?"

"We could do that," he agreed grimly, "but it might not work. I do not know how far the... explosion will travel. It may be that no place is safe. Besides, it is my responsibility. I feel I must try. It is not right to leave these innocent people to die. They are not my enemies, nor the children of my enemies, and I wish them no harm. I must try to do this. I must try to prevent the rupture."

The pair fell silent, contemplating the grim scenario and wishing for a better option.

"So, we must part ways then?" Violet asked at last, turning to Leontios and finding him staring at her in contemplation. "What? I must stay and wait for my father. You must go and try to save everyone."

"You could help me," he suggested. "You have an affinity to the moon. You called to it, remember?

117

In the desert. The clouds obeyed you. You could act as my priestess."

"Do you think I could?" Violet asked. The thought of taking part in an archaic ritual thrilled her, and since her belief in Leontios's story still was far from settled, it was the kind of thrill she had felt riding in an automobile or diving into a pool: mostly safe and with only a hint of risk. Still, she didn't like the idea of her father arriving—after being held hostage and with who knows what kind of injuries—and not being there to meet him.

How could I do that to him? She could picture him, bewildered at hearing she would be at the hotel waiting and then arriving to find no one there. *Especially if he's injured, which is probable given how violently we derailed. He's frailer and was further forward toward the impact.*

But what if he doesn't come back? The thought hurt, and yet, she had to consider it. *He's an elderly man. Over seventy now. His heart has acted strangely for years. He even needs medicine for it. Will the freedom fighters allow a hostage to take medicine if he has an attack? Will he be able to manage to get to our cabin and dig his pills out of the luggage before he succumbs? And that doesn't even consider the possibility of outright violence.*

"I think, VioletWarren," Leontios said solemnly, drawing her out of her sad ruminations and back into their conversation, "that I have a better chance of success with you than without you."

"Oh, but Father," she protested aloud, not sure what she wanted him to say in response.

"Honestly," he replied, "if we do not drain the crystal in time, neither of you will survive. The next best thing I can do for you is to remove you from your body, so you do not feel the pain of dying. For your father, I can do nothing."

He was so earnest and so serious, it made her heart pound. *It doesn't make sense, but what if he's right? What if there is a threat? What if he can help? What if I can help him save everyone? Save the antiquities I love?* She looked deep into his eyes, into the warm, hypnotic gaze that made her want to believe the impossible. Almost without thought, her mouth formed the words, "I will try to help you in any way I can. If Father is well, he will be brought to the hotel and wait. He likes to drink tea and read newspapers in exotic places. Even shopping strains his interest. If he... if he didn't survive the attack..." She gulped. "If that is what happened, well, sitting here won't help him anyway."

Leontios nodded, exhaling heavily, so his breath blew a strand of golden-brown hair that had escaped her chignon away from her forehead. "I am glad of your help, VioletWarren. In truth, I think you may be the only one who can. At least in this age."

She smiled, a thin curving of her lips that she knew did not match the crimping of her eyes or wrinkling of her forehead.

His hand lifted, touched her face and traced a line down her cheek.

She closed her eyes, leaning into his hand. He cupped her face. Again, Violet pursed her lips, eager to taste his kiss.

"We should leave as soon as possible," Leontios said, his voice tender. "At sunset tonight if we are able."

Violet opened her eyes and looked at him. He had not withdrawn from their intense connection. His eyes bored into hers with the same heat as always, but he did not bring her face close. Instead, his hand dropped, touching the tips of his fingers to the tips of hers.

"Do you have any conveyance in this world of yours that is faster than walking?"

Violet nodded, drawing her fingers away from his and drumming them nervously on the table. "Maybe. If I can find a driver with a car or carriage, we could hire him to take us to the edge of town. That will take at least some time off our trip. Maybe further, depending on the existence of roads."

"I do not know what that means," Leontios said, "but I am willing to trust you." And yet, he looked disappointed.

Violet bit her lip, wondering what to make of his

expression. "Very well. I will try to find someone who can drive us as far as we can go. Do you at least have a direction in mind?"

"Southwest, in the main," he replied. "However, it is not directly southwest. There are several strategic turns along the way, all marked by rock formations that may no longer be present. Also, I have only traveled the route once, and it was when I was a child."

Violet shook her head. "Daunting, to say the least."

"Excuse me," a gently accented voice interrupted the intense conversation.

Violet looked up to see the waiter who had served her soup earlier that day. "Yes? Can I help you?"

"No, madame," the young man replied, "but perhaps I can help you. Did I hear you say you needed to hire a car and driver?"

Violet nodded.

"I happen to have inherited a car from a distant relative, and sometimes, when I'm not working at the restaurant, I drive people around the city. Reasonable price."

"How fortuitous," Violet said cautiously. "It seems a good solution. Is it a reliable car?"

"Yes, ma'am," the gentleman replied.

Violet glanced at Leontios and found him studying the young Egyptian with close attention.

"Do you think this might be a good option?" she asked him.

"Perhaps." He narrowed his eyes, and the tattoos on his temples rolled on a sea of crow's feet.

For a moment, Violet's heart clenched. *I've known this man two days. I shouldn't feel more than a passing attraction, and yet... He's intelligent, otherworldly and wildly handsome. Those eyes. My God.*

She shook off her distraction, looking again at Leontios. This time he met her gaze, sending a jolt straight to her core.

"Let us take a moment to gather our thoughts and resources," Leontios suggested, "and return to confirm with you later. Please give us..." He spoke a term Violet did not understand.

"Pardon?" The waiter turned to her.

"Two hours," Violet guessed. "Give us two hours, please, for the heat of the day to pass." She grinned. "I'm not bred for Egypt's climate."

"It is unusually hot for March. The Khamsin is nasty this year."

"Ah, yes. I remember reading about that," Violet agreed. "I was hoping to find a comfortable temperature in contrast to the cold back home. Looks like I made a mistake."

"Tourists!" The waiter rolled his eyes heavenward.

"I know," Violet agreed. "I made a mistake, but I must press on. The effort and expense I put into this trip cannot go to waste, hot wind notwithstanding. So, since that is the case, I appreciate your help. What is your name, sir, in case we need to ask for you?"

"I am called Azaan, ma'am," the young man informed her, "and if you ask for me at the desk, they will find me. My shift in the restaurant ends shortly, but I will wait for you. I'm also familiar with the marketplace near here. I can help you find supplies if you need them." He spoke to Violet, but his gaze fixed on Leontios. He inhaled deeply through his nose as though considering something he had not shared.

"Thank you." Violet found that her hand was again touching Leontios's, the pads of their fingers pressed together.

Azaan wandered away, untying his apron as he went. Leontios's fingers changed position, lacing through Violet's and urging her upright as he got to his feet.

"Where are we going?" she asked.

"Do you have a private place where we can talk?" he asked.

Heads turned around the restaurant.

Violet's face burned at the thought of all those strangers speculating, but there was no hope for it. "Come with me."

She led him out of the dining room and through the lobby, up the stairs—so many stairs—to the wood and white box of a bedroom where she had passed her restless daytime sleep. Though she knew it to be entirely inappropriate to have a strange man in her bedroom, she couldn't feel wrong about it. Somehow, in their brief acquaintance, Leontios had become as vital to her as her own heart. She could scarcely imagine spending another day without him. As though, in a single day, he had become family. *As though he's been my companion for years. Like… my book.* She pushed the thought away and urged him to a seat in a small armchair with rich blue upholstery in the corner.

"Is this wise, VioletWarren?" he asked after staring at her for a long, silent moment.

"Why would it not be?" Violet asked as she perched on the edge of the bed. "Did your other-worldly senses tell you something untrustworthy about this young man?"

"I am not sure," Leontios replied, eyes narrowed. "I could almost swear I know him. But that makes no sense. Apart from you, everyone I know has been dead for several millennia."

"True. And he did not seem familiar to me, though I only 'know' a handful of people in Egypt —all passing acquaintances. Perhaps he's a many generations descendant?"

"Perhaps. At any rate, that would make no difference. No memory of my people could possibly exist in this era."

"I can attest to it," Violet agreed. "Not to put on any airs, but I'm aware of at least a bit about most if not all of the ancient civilizations currently known, and I'm particularly educated on Egyptian antiquities. I have never read about or heard of Skeon. If any knowledge existed, I would like to think I know of it."

"Likely you would. I suspect that King Djoser, having heard of his defeat at Skeon and the city's utter disappearance, declined to record his failure for the ages."

"That's typical of Egyptian kings," Violet agreed. "So, unless you have reason to think Azaan is up to no good, help navigating the souk and a car ride as far as the road can take us will be beneficial."

"I will have to rely on your expertise, as I have no understanding of what you are describing," he concurred, steepling his fingers in front of his lips and leaning his elbows on his knees.

"What supplies do you think we will need?" Violet asked. "After our impromptu trek through the desert last night, I don't want to go *anywhere* without at least water canteens and a head covering. A change of clothes would also be welcome. I'm not dressed quite right. We should also bring some kind of lamp. It's dark out there, away from the city, and if we must still travel for more than a day, it's best to move at night. Especially as this seems to be an unusually hot March."

"You are correct all on all counts," Leontios agreed. "The hot spring winds are painful this year. How can we procure water skins, head coverings and… lamps? What is that?"

"A device for lighting our way at night," she explained.

"Ah," Leontios replied. "I would have said torches."

"No doubt you would have," she agreed. "A lamp is just a torch inside a windowed box. It protects the flame from wind and rain and the carrier from soot and ash."

"A modern marvel," Leontios said, a gentle irony in his voice. "Shall we rest for a time, until the heat of the day passes, and then reconnect with our guide?"

Violet nodded and rose to her feet. Her pulse pounded in her neck as she approached the chair and the strange man who had burst into her life, unexpected yet irresistible, only the day before.

He stood before her, slim and stately, his dark eyes boring down into hers. He reached out one hand and paused, waiting.

Violet bit her lip, reaching out and laying her palm in his. Her fingers laced through his, urging him closer.

His expression changed from intensity to puzzlement.

What are you asking? Violet wondered, letting her confusion contort her face. *I shouldn't want you to kiss me, but I do. Why does that confuse you, Leo? What do you want from me?*

"I will return to the bed supplied for me. There does not seem to be room here for both of us, and this chair is far from comfortable."

Unsure what to make of his comments, let alone his unreadable expression, Violet felt herself wilting. "Yes, I suppose."

CHAPTER 9

Two hours later, Leontios and Violet stepped out of the hotel. Azaan already stood on the front stoop, his back to the river that fronted the hotel, regarding them with an idle posture that belied his intense gaze.

Violet studied him, trying to understand what he thought he was seeing. *A couple of tourists planning something foolish and ill-advised, no doubt. He's probably wondering how much money he can get from us before we wander off to our doom.* "Where do we begin?"

"That depends," Azaan replied. "What do you want to purchase?"

Violet pondered briefly. "Clothing suitable to rough going. This dress isn't doing me any favors.

A lantern. Food that won't spoil in the heat over several days. Containers for water."

"I will also need a means of carrying goods," Leontios added. "Miss Warren should not carry the entire burden."

"I know just where to go," Azaan said. "Follow me. I hope you don't mind a bit of a walk. My car is too large to take into these narrow streets, and it attracts too much attention."

"Understandable," Violet said. "I have no trouble walking. It's better for taking in the ambiance anyway."

"Follow me," the young man urged, setting off at a brisk pace. The area around the hotel, with its tidy streets and towering palms, called up images of luxury and foreignness that seemed both familiar and somehow wrong. They passed another large structure. "The British Embassy," Azaan called over his shoulder. "But you are not British, are you, ma'am?"

Violet didn't answer. She was too busy looking at the gleaming white two-story building with its overly watered lawn. *They never just let things be, do they? It always has to look like home.* Shaking her head, she followed their guide inland, along streets that grew narrower and less manicured. In time, the scenery began to match her expectations, based on photos she'd pored over back in Pittsburgh. She found herself in a row of small shops tucked under the overhangs of larger buildings, some with awnings that partially shielded the merchants from the slanted late-day sun.

The first shop consisted of a messily charming cluster of ceramic and metalwork objects, including a huge quantity of brass lamps hanging from the rafters.

"Hello," Violet said in Arabic to the veiled woman who busied herself in rubbing street dust off the gently gleaming lamps.

The woman lifted her chin and regarded Violet curiously.

"What is the purpose of these lamps?"

The woman tilted her head. "They are for Muslim ceremonies. I do not sell them to foreigners seeking curiosities, though I will tell you of another merchant who will if you like."

"Oh, no!" Violet protested. "I would never dream of it. Do you have anything suitable to light a traveler's way at night?"

The woman considered her another minute. Though the sequined garment that veiled her face prevented Violet from seeing her mouth, a crinkling at the corners of her eyes suggested a smile. "Because you have some manners, unlike your countrymen, and because you speak my language instead of demanding I speak yours, I will show you something useful." She ducked behind a curtain in a deep, vibrant shade of blue, stitched with metallic gold geometric shapes, and emerged with…"

"Is that a *battery-operated* lantern?" Violet asked.

The woman nodded. "Much more reliable than oil, and much sturdier. It will light your way."

"Batteries don't last long, though," Violet pointed out. "I can bring a supply of oil. Can you supply an additional battery?"

"Sadly, I cannot," the merchant replied. "But I do not have traveling lamps here, as you can see. This came to me by accident, and I'm happy to part with it if you want it. If not, if you want a different kind of lantern, I will direct you to someone else."

"One moment," Violet requested.

At the woman's nod, she turned to Leontios. "She has a kind of lamp that might be useful. The fuel cannot spill because it is contained in… in a kind of metal housing. Other lamps are fueled with oil, which we would need to procure, and which might spill if I tripped or if a sandstorm blew up. However, it will not last long. What do you think?"

Leontios screwed his lips to the side. "Based on the moon we saw last night, I think we will not need light for our journey, even at the height of darkness, unless it becomes cloudy. It is also windy, which will discourage clouds from gathering. Per- haps it would be best to bring this… lantern? Yes, lantern she offers. That is unless you think we should bring both."

Violet looked around for Azaan, who had removed himself across the narrow street to chat with a man selling hookahs. He seemed out of earshot, so she said, sotto voce, "I'm not sure how much our other supplies will weigh. We don't want to be overloaded with something we don't need. You say your city is how far from here?"

He shrugged. "I cannot say without knowing where King Djoser's pyramid is. After we reach it, at least one full night's walk. Most likely more because it will take time to find the entrance. Two to three days, stopping once the heat becomes dangerous, I would guess. Maybe more."

Violet nodded, her mind busily untangling the puzzle. "I think this lady's lantern would be best then. It's a relatively short time, with a bright moon and the possibility of heavy winds."

"I will trust your judgment," Leontios agreed.

I hope your trust is not misplaced, Violet thought. *I'm far from certain.*

He took her hand and gently squeezed. "All will be well, VioletWarren. The sun and the moon are with us."

Violet nodded. Turning back to the eagerly waiting merchant, she said. "I will take the battery lantern if the price is affordable."

The woman raised one eyebrow, which made the sequins on her veil clatter. "Then let us bargain."

Ten minutes later, Violet and Leontios left the shop carrying the lantern by the ring affixed to the top of a pentagon of glass panels.

Azaan hurried over to them, scrutinizing their purchase. "I hope you did not let her gouge you too much," he commented.

An Arabic insult floated to them on a hot, dusty wind, showing that the merchant woman spoke more English than she'd let on.

"It was a most satisfactory negotiation," Violet replied primly. "What's next, Azaan?"

"Follow me. I know where to find a food shop and a clothing shop near each other." He hurried away again. Violet had to trot to keep up.

A series of twists and turns led them deep into the heart of the souk, where the scent of cumin and cardamom hung heavy in the air. "And now, my friends, I must leave you to prepare the car. You can find the rest of what you need in this area. Just meet me back at the hotel." He ducked out of sight.

Violet frowned. "How does he think we'll be able to do that?" she asked. "I have long since lost track of where we are. Leontios, do you recall the way?" She looked around at the crowded cubicles, each one housing different exotic or practical wares to tempt both travelers and locals. Clothing. Metalwork. Textiles. Papyri. The tight-clustered commotion made Violet feel a bit dizzy, as though she was inside one of her father's clanking, bustling steel mills.

Hawkers shouted in a blend of Arabic and English, advertising their products to the street before them. A mob of men, women and children—some brown-skinned and others British pale—trotted around them.

A tempting scent of honey and roasted nuts attracted Violet's attention one way until a rough shout in Arabic, "Dried fish!" turned her around. She placed her hands on her ears and closed her eyes to block out the wild stimulation.

A warm hand closed on her wrist, and she opened her eyes to see Leontios looking at her in concern. "I believe I can get us back to the hotel," he said, "but leaving us here was not wise. A less aware person might well be lost."

"Then I'm glad to be with you," she said.

He grinned with one side of his mouth and reached for her hand. She laced their fingers together.

"So, what do we need now, VioletWarren?"

"Let's start with some proper adventuring clothing for me. That looks like a second-hand shop over there. They may have a satchel for you as well. Then we can fill both with food from the various meat and pita sellers I see over there." She pointed straight ahead, where enticing aromas of sausages and bread wafted into the street. "As long as we don't make any more turns, are you sure you can get us back?"

"I am growing in confidence as I ponder. So long as we stay on this particular road, we will not become lost."

"Let's move along then," Violet urged. "There's precious little sunlight left, and I feel a cold breeze creeping in."

"The desert will be colder at night. We must prepare for it, or we will be most uncomfortable," he warned.

"So I have heard," Violet agreed. "Come on." Tugging on his hand, she led him into the nearest clothing shop.

Despite their best efforts, the procuring of supplies took over an hour as the temperature dropped and the light faded. Violet and Leontios at last made their way to the front of the Shepheard hotel, where the crimson light fell in a blinding shaft.

"Ow," she complained, shielding her eyes and squinting. "I hope our ride is ready. I've walked enough for one day."

"Oh, you're here!" Azaan's familiar voice floated to her ears.

She turned to glare. "Just find our way back to the hotel, eh?"

His habitual, penetrating stare transformed in an instant into a look of excessive innocence. "Did you have any trouble? It's not that hard to find your way out of the souk. You didn't get lost, did you?"

"We did not," Leontios said sternly, pursing his lips at the young man, "but I do not think playing tricks on people is a good way to ingratiate yourself to strangers."

"It's a pity," Violet added. "I was going to add a generous tip to your fee. Now, I don't know if I should." As she spoke, her vision finally adjusted to the brightness, and she saw something she would never have expected. "Oh, my word," she breathed. "Is that a…"

"Bugatti Type 18," Azaan replied, grinning. "I modified it to add the rear bench behind the seats, as I'm rarely transporting just one person." He patted the shiny black hood, drawing Violet's gaze back to the blinding light reflecting off the paint and chrome.

"It's beautiful," she said reverently. "I'm a bit afraid, Azaan, that I can't afford a ride in such a fancy car. How much will you want to take us to the southwest edge of town?"

"Don't worry," the young man replied. "I know how much I can afford to charge. It's a fancy car, but in the end, a ride is just a ride. I won't gouge you… much." He winked.

Violet laughed and hefted her satchel, which

now weighed more than it had before with the addition of several essential items. "Come on, Leo. Let's go."

Leontios looked askance at the car. He scowled, the tattoos rolling on the skin of his temples.

"What's wrong with him?" Azaan asked.

"Oh, he's from a remote part of, um, Mexico. He's not used to cars," Violet explained.

"I pity him." Azaan gave Leontios a hard look.

"I think he will be quite nervous at the speed," Violet went on. "I'd better sit with him on the rear bench. You don't mind, do you?"

Azaan laughed. "Not what I had hoped," he looked Violet up and down, "but I will let you serve… your servant?" His tone turned suggestive, teasing Violet and urging her to argue with him.

"Fine," Violet agreed easily. She scrambled over the side of the open-topped vehicle and perched in the flat sheet of upholstered wood that had been bolted onto the chassis behind the two bucket seats. "Come on, Leo," she urged again, patting the seat beside her.

Scowling, Leontios made his way over to the car and tentatively climbed up onto the bench.

Azaan spent another minute, his hand sheltering his eyes from the sun, looking from Violet to Leontios as though trying to understand what he was seeing. Then he shook his head hard, vaulted into the seat and pushed the button.

The Bugatti started with a guttural snarl. Azaan eased it away from the curb, nudging his way carefully into the wild traffic of pedestrians, animals and a few other cars making their way down the streets of Cairo. A horn emitted a loud honk. A donkey brayed. A voice shouted ugly words in Arabic that made Violet's face burn.

The snarl grew louder as their speed increased.

Leontios grabbed at Violet's hand. She turned to look and blinked to see his face dead white. His fingers trembled harder than the car vibrated. *Poor man. This is difficult for me, and I've been in a car before. Leo is so bewildered by technology.*

They eased into a thick stream of traffic and crossed a river. *It's the Nile,* she realized. *I'm actually crossing the Nile right now!* The sunset sparkled on the lovely blue water, and Violet could easily envision Cleopatra floating along in her barge.

Her companion seemed less excited and more... terrified.

She leaned close and spoke directly into his ear to be sure he would hear over the noise. "Are you all right?"

He shook his head. "It is unnatural to move at such speed."

She grinned. "Welcome to the twentieth century."

"Century of what?" he shot back.

She shrugged. "I can explain if you'd like, but

not while we're driving," she replied. "There's too much, and it's too loud."

He nodded.

She slid her fingers between his, enjoying the warmth of his palm. Almost without thought, her thumb slipped over his.

Leontios moved his thumb out and trapped hers under his. It felt strangely erotic as if the hold of finger on finger mirrored much more intimate caresses. He confirmed the image, stroking her the way she had him.

He wants me, too, she realized. *It doesn't make sense, but it's so real. The realist thing I've ever felt.*

Through the crowded streets, they eased past boxy reddish-brown buildings interspersed with spires, minarets and palm trees. People dressed in robes dodged among the traffic. Soldiers in sand-colored British fatigues regarded the crowd with bored expressions. Egyptian forces in red fez hats scowled in disapproval at the British. Though no one showed aggression, Violet could feel the tension in the air, palpable as an electrical current. *Peace is not to be found in this place. Father and I made a serious miscalculation, and it had nothing to do with the weather. I wonder if the vacation part of this vacation will ever arrive.*

The Bugatti made a sharp right turn onto a wider, even busier road. They increased speed to match the pace of the traffic. The bench on which they sat wobbled and swayed on too few bolts as they rattled and bumped along the uneven places in the street. Cars and carts careened into the stream carelessly, causing them to swerve. Violet clutched harder at Leontios's hand, no longer confident in the safety of the fancy automobile. Bouncing along on the back felt nothing like sitting inside a vehicle. *If we fell, no one would be able to stop in time to avoid trampling us.* Her free hand clamped down on the edge of the seat, and her knees tightened around it as well.

"Further south," Leontios shouted over the roar of the engine. "Not quite so far to the west."

Azaan nodded and executed a sharp left, inciting shouts and honks as he pushed his way through the lanes of oncoming traffic onto a smaller street.

Here, he was able to reduce speed, and Violet released a shaky breath. "This is terrible," she murmured, hoping their driver would not overhear.

Leontios stroked her thumb with his again. Despite her nerves, the gentle touch elicited a riot of tingles that shot straight to her belly.

"How long will this go on?" Leontios asked.

"Probably longer than you'd think," Violet replied. "Cairo is quite large."

He nodded, the corners of his mouth crimped tight with discomfort.

Violet's prediction proved correct. Long minutes

passed as they careened through the streets, dodging slower vehicles and pedestrians, slowly working their way south and west at Leontios's shouted instructions until the buildings thinned and spread, transforming from central multistory structures to homes and small shops. A shape loomed in the distance, and Violet sucked in a sharp breath. An echoing gasp matched hers.

"VioletWarren, is this the structure I saw as a child?"

She shook her head. "No, Leo. It's not. That one is further south. After King Djoser made his pyramid, many of his descendants also thought it was a good idea."

He nodded. "I think I should see the original one. It might help me understand… what I'm looking for."

She dipped her chin, acknowledging his comment, but at the same time, noting that their driver had leaned back slightly in his seat, his ear inclined toward them.

He doesn't need to know too much, she thought, not certain what harm this eavesdropper could possibly cause. A thin, silvery whisper that transcended reason warned her not to say too much. She didn't try to argue it away.

"Well, friends, this is as far as I go," Azaan said, pulling to a stop along the curb in front of a noisy tavern. "The roads get too bumpy for my car if we continue. If you'd like a ride into the desert… perhaps to the pyramids? I have a cousin who rents out camels. I can summon him in the morning."

"I'm not sure," Violet said, again noting how his gaze lingered, narrow and squinty, on Leontios's face. "Can we call for you tomorrow if we need to? Or would you give us the name so we can ask after him if needed?"

"Perhaps. Are you sure you want to risk not having access?" Azaan clambered out of the Bugatti and offered Violet a hand.

"To you?" Violet raised an eyebrow as she jumped to the ground. "Easy on the hard sell, Mister. The pyramids are nearby. I am quite sure there are camels and donkeys and guides aplenty. No need to pretend we'll be stranded without your help." She opened her bag and retrieved some bills, which she handed to Azaan.

The man's lips grinned, but his eyes hardened. He tilted his head slightly to the side and scrutinized… Violet's handbag. "Ah, but without my advice, you may get swindled. Not every guide is honest."

"We will take that risk," Leontios said, jumping down from the impromptu guest seat, his newly acquired satchel swinging with the movement. "Thank you for your assistance this evening, and I wish you a good night." Taking Violet's hand, he led her away.

She allowed it.

A soft curse carried on a warm evening breeze.

"It is still too hot to venture into the desert," Leontios said. "While I hate to delay a minute, dying of thirst and sun is not pleasant. Perhaps we can pass an hour here in this place? What is this place?"

"A bar," Violet replied, "and if your country had any kind of shops, you must know what that means."

He nodded, eyes seeming to read a document she couldn't see. "A place that offers strong drinks and perhaps some food?"

Violet nodded. "If Skeon isn't a Muslim country, which I'm sure it's not since you do not know what that means..." she imitated his unique word formations in a gentle gest, "I assume your people do not follow the ban against alcohol?"

He grinned, showing white teeth. "If you mean do we enjoy beer on frequent occasions or some wine at celebrations, we do."

She shook her head. *The Egyptians—the ancient Egyptians—also enjoyed wine and beer. How very different from modern Egypt.* The evidence that his wild tale might have some truth to it caused a strange, squirming sensation to arise in her belly.

"Well, that would be one way to pass the time." She glanced around at the pale faces and buff-colored uniforms clustered around them, of men either seated at tables, standing in conversation or leaning on walls observing the scene.

"You there!" a voice shouted. "We don't allow Egyptians in here."

Violet turned to see the bartender, a hefty man with curly mutton chops. He scowled, pointing at Leontios.

"I am not Egyptian," he snarled.

"I surely hope not. Lady, if you're sneaking off with this guy…" he looked askance at their joined hands.

Violet pasted a charming smile on her face. "Of course not," she replied. "As my husband says, he's not Egyptian. He's Mexican, and we're here on our honeymoon."

"Bad timing, if you don't mind my saying so," the bartender replied, leaning back, his shoulders relaxing. "The grippe is waning, but it's still out there, it's hot as blazes, and if I'm not very much mistaken, the whole country is about to go up like a powder keg."

"So I discovered, a bit too late. News takes *such* a long time to reach us in the United States, and I've been so busy with wedding preparations, I didn't have time to pay attention to what did get through, not once the Great War ended. But, you know, here we are. Might as well see the pyramids since we've come all this way."

The man shrugged. "I suppose. You'd better be careful out there, Miss… Miss…"

"Missus. Warren." Violet batted her eyelashes and released Leontios's hand, instead wrapping her arm around his. This close, she could take in the scent of his skin. No sweat, strangely, but a blend of spicy cologne, enticing arousal and paper. "Um… ahem. Yes. We'll be very careful. Thanks for the warning."

She glanced at her companion as though besotted and saw him curl up one corner of his mouth in amusement.

"So, you know, he doesn't speak English that well. We mostly use his native language to communicate. But he did tell me just now that he'd like a glass of beer, and… I might go for one myself."

The bartender chuckled. "Choose a seat. I'll bring your drinks right out."

Violet took Leontios's arm, leading him to a table in the corner. She selected a dark, shadowed space far from the chatting soldiers. "Pull the chair back from the table," she breathed.

Leontios dropped her arm and obeyed. She sank down, trapping his fingers against the wood, and scooted herself forward. Then she indicated the other chair with a subtle gesture of her head. He sat.

"VioletWarren," Leontios said softly, "why did

you tell these people that I am your husband? It is best to be honest with people."

"I know," she replied, closing her eyes in frustration. "I generally favor the truth myself. It's easier to remember. However, the 'truth' of our current situation is so far from plausible that I didn't dare mention it."

He conceded with a nod. "I agree that the truth, in this case, would be difficult to swallow. However, husband? Why that?"

"Well, for one," she explained, toying with the edge of the tablecloth, "you don't carry yourself like a manservant. You have the demeanor of the brother of a king."

"Ah. That is true," he agreed, arresting her nervous movement with a hand on hers.

"And we can't seem to stop touching either," she added, indicating their entwined fingers. "For a 'lady,' this sort of touching would be unseemly and deeply suspicious, particularly if the man in question is a servant. It's easier to let them think we're married."

"Is marriage common then?"

She nodded. "it's basically the only way a woman like myself—who isn't that young—to be considered fully respectable. It's rare for anyone to choose a single life, which I have. Especially when I've had offers. I didn't prefer any of those men."

"I wonder," he said thoughtfully…

But before he could say what he wondered, the taverner approached with two mugs of beer.

Violet squeezed his hand and began to speak in ancient Egyptian, hoping he would understand and be able to respond. "Remember that our friend here thinks you do not speak English. Can you communicate in the language of your enemies?"

"I can," Leontios agreed in words she could barely understand, so differently did he pronounce them.

Two cool glasses of beer slid across the table. Violet arrested hers before it could fall onto the floor and lifted it, hiding a smile in a deep sip. Leontios mirrored the movements.

"Are you sure you want to go out into the desert at night?" the bartender asked. "It might not be safe. Besides, despite the heatwave, it is sure to be uncomfortably cold."

"I'll be ready," Violet said, her voice growing cold as she patted her handbag. Inside, her derringer clunked against first her crystal and then her water canteen. She raised one eyebrow.

"Oho, that sort, are you? Well, I wish you luck, you and your fella. Have a happy honeymoon. I'll bring you some sandwiches on the house."

"Thank you," Violet said primly as he scooted away, stroking his sideburn.

"This man is too inquisitive," Leontios pointed out.

"He is," Violet agreed. "He's probably just bored, but that doesn't mean he needs to scrutinize our business."

Leontios drank some of his beer, then lowered the glass and looked at it quizzically.

"Taste different?" she asked.

"Rather yes. I have never had cold beer before. It is enjoyable."

Violet grinned. "It's strange," she said, thinking aloud, "that while everything we're doing is dangerous. While I'm still so very worried about my father, this is the sort of adventure I came here to have. Not just to stare at antiquities like all the tourists. I want to experience another time as a participant. I have always longed for that."

"Then I am glad I can share it with you. I wish I could bring to you Skeon as it was in its heyday. It was so beautiful. A blue and green oasis surrounded by the whitest sand. Date palms. Grapevines. Wheatfields." He paused in his recitation to sip his drink again, and a soft half-smile graced his thin lips. "I would have loved to share it with you. I think you would have appreciated it there."

"I know I would," Violet breathed, "if you were there with me." The images played out behind her eyes as though she had been there before. *It was my dream,* she recalled as the hazy, half-forgotten images sharpened in her memory. *I dreamed I was in*

Skeon with Leontios. I dreamed he touched me. And in fact, he was touching her. His hand remained in hers, warm and gentle. His callouses caressed her skin. She longed for him to kiss her in a way she'd never wanted a kiss before. He sounded and smelled and *felt* so good, she wanted nothing more than to taste him. To embed him in her senses. In the core of her being. In her every experience.

Leontios set down his beer and turned fully toward her, staring deep into her eyes as he caressed her hand with tender, gentle strokes.

Why won't you kiss me? She longed to wail, but her endless training in proper behavior choked the words in her throat.

He looked steadily but made no move toward her face. At last, Violet gave up in frustration, breaking the intense eye contact and taking a large gulp of her drink. "Do you think it has cooled enough to leave soon?"

"It has. Finish your drink and let us be on our way."

She nodded, defeated. *I must be imagining his interest. Surely, he would have done something about it by now if he wanted to.*

CHAPTER 10

A huge, fat moon hung low overhead, full as a pregnant belly, beaming its soft golden light onto the white, white sand.

They stood in the shadow of Djoser's ruined step pyramid. "This is the pyramid you saw as a child," Violet explained. Breathing deeply after a three-hour walk from the outskirts of Cairo, she dusted sandy fragments off her new-to-her men's trousers and dirty tan shirt. *Not pretty, but practical,* she thought. *I wonder what Leontios thinks of them… if anything.* He had shown no reaction to the sight of her in pants. Her friends in Pittsburgh would have been scandalized.

Leontios sucked in a deep breath and released it. "I suddenly can feel the years. They are heavy on me as on this poor ruin. Ah, Violet, it was so lovely and new. So fascinatingly different. I had never seen such a large, manmade structure in my life, and there it was, standing like a giant over the desert. It spoke of the power of the king and also of the power of human creativity."

"You're quite lyrical when you're in the mood to be," she pointed out.

"If you had read my book," he said, "you would have seen that, well, I enjoy manipulating words."

"I guessed that about you. I wish I had had the chance to read it once I got the translation disc. Your language is challenging, even with help. I only read the first page."

His white grin flashed in the darkness. "You can know anything you would like. Only ask me. I will tell my tales and share my secrets, Violet, with you only."

She smiled back, but his answer confused her. *I could swear he's falling for me. The things he says. The way he won't let go of my hand. And yet… I don't understand the message.*

"Where do we go from here?" she asked, not sure whether she meant literally or whether she wanted him to confirm his feelings.

Leontios, of course, took the question literally. "We must continue southwest. Is the… the lantern ready?"

"It's ready whenever the need arises," Violet replied. She lifted the metal ring, holding the lantern before them. "Though I don't think we'll need it unless some clouds blow up. I wish there were a path to follow. Trekking through the desert, even by bright moonlight, seems like a good way to die."

"I agree. I would not suggest it if the need were not dire."

"Well, then, Leontios, please lead the way. If it will take us all night or longer to find your home, we'd better get going."

He started off. Violet trudged after him, stumbling in the pyramid's deep shadow. Outside the pyramid complex, the moon shone bright. Her free hand remained laced with his, palm to palm, the pulses in their wrists throbbing in unison.

Stepping out of the shadow of the irregular pile of stacked, crumbling boxes, they looked cautiously around. Humanity milled here and there in pointless busy-ness. Off in the distance, they saw an encampment. Probably treasure hunters. British soldiers approached, loudly challenging the campers.

Suddenly nervous, Violet shied away.

"What is wrong, VioletWarren?" Leontios asked.

"What if someone questions us?" she suggested. "Remember, you look Egyptian, even if you're not, and there's a lot of unrest. What if they assume you're on your way out of town to meet with rebels? We could be shot."

She tugged him back into the shadow of the pyramid, where they would be less visible. Sand crunched softly under her boots.

"What do you suggest?" Leontios asked.

Violet shrugged. "Under normal circumstances, I would probably approach the whole group and plead for assistance. Claim with wide-eyed innocence to be an adventurer wanting to do some preposterous thing. Bat my eyelashes and simper. In a group, they won't be able to do me much harm, but… they cannot help with this task. I'm not asking to see the pyramid or get into some dark tomb. What could I say? I want to venture into the trackless desert looking for something I don't know how to find?"

"Then sneaking away without attracting attention is the best option?"

She nodded. "I don't know if we can pull it off, though."

"Could we not say, if we are stopped, that we are lovers seeking privacy? That we wanted to see the pyramid by night because it is romantic, and we only wish to step behind a dune and be alone together for an hour?"

Violet gulped. "They would assume… many things."

"You have already presented me as your husband," he pointed out.

"And I already regret it," she added. "I don't

think the bartender believed us, and in these circumstances…"

"They will assume you are a hostage?"

She nodded.

"That would be a reasonable conclusion from their perspective, I suppose. Then you must go alone. If you are caught—a woman alone—you can pretend to be an outrageous adventurer doing something foolish, and they will believe you."

"What are you saying?" she hissed louder than was wise. "How can I go without you? *You* barely know where we're going. I can't go alone. That's insane. This whole thing is insane. I should go back to Cairo and wait for my father."

"Violet, no…" Leontios grasped her elbow. "Listen to me. It would not make sense for you to go alone. This is true. I only mean for you to get away from all these people alone. Then, when you are clear of their eyes…"

"How does that even make sense?" she demanded. "If I go alone, where will you be?"

"I will be with you."

She frowned.

"I can transform back into the book. Put me in your satchel and carry me out of this area—head straight south. Do you see the large dune there?" he pointed.

Violet raised one eyebrow.

"Go there. Go behind it. If there is no one in

sight, call me back. You know how. Read the invocation on the first page. I will return to my human form."

Violet frowned harder. She could feel her whole face dragging downward. *Probably creating new wrinkles,* she thought lamely. Now, at this moment, she had to face that either the man she'd been flirting with, who had truly saved her from the attack on the train and its aftermath, who had shown her magic tricks, and who had an unsettling effect on her libido, was either crazy or... Even now, her mind veered away from the thought. *How can a man, a living, vital man, be a book? It defies rationality.*

Her heart didn't want to be rational. It wanted to grab big handfuls of his clothing and bury her face in his chest, drawing his essence into herself. Read the tattoos she knew must be hiding under his clothing as she traced them with her fingers. She did not want to see him as a book. She also did not want to see his delusion revealed.

"I don't want to do that," she whispered, dropping his hand and turning away.

"Then you should quickly come up with another plan. This is your world, VioletWarren. Your time. We must get away from these people. We must get out into the desert. I must, because only I know the way. You must because only you know this time. We cannot go together because we will be seen, and I, who look like an Egyptian, will likely be killed before you can come up with a lie strong enough to protect me. You can get through alone more easily as you are smaller than I. Lighter. Slighter. You can also lie your way out of trouble if you are alone. How else can you get me out of the vicinity without arousing the suspicions of these warriors who are already on edge?"

Violet bit her lip. Tears stung her eyes, and she blinked hard to clear them. "I do not want to do this," she repeated.

"But we must. I am trusting you, VioletWarren. Once I am transformed, only you have the knowledge and power to bring me back. I will be an insensible book until you revive me." He held out one hand and, as before, touched his palm and the tips of his fingers to hers. He waited, holding his breath. Violet sobbed and laced her fingers through his.

Her hand closed on air.

A soft thump sounded, and she looked down. Her breath caught in her throat as she saw the familiar book she'd loved for so many years. The brilliant paint. The etched leather. The crackly papyrus pages sitting unevenly within the cover. She knew its every nuance. She stooped and gathered the beloved treasure against her chest. Tears escaped her lashes, streaming down her cheeks unchecked even as she schooled her breathing to silence.

There was no room in her satchel for the book, nor in Leontios's, which lay in the sand nearly forgotten. Unable to handle both bags, the book and the lantern safely, she unbuckled the strap of her satchel and fed the lantern's upper ring through, fastening it up again so the lamp hung along her back. She angled the other bag's strap over her shoulder so it lay against her opposite hip. Thus, she left both hands free to clutch the book tight to her chest, the leather soft and warm as flesh.

She turned to glance at the encampment where soldiers and adventurers shouted at each other in British accents. Their contention had grown so loud that the random figures she'd seen milling around the pyramid had all turned to stare. Violet crept again out from behind the pyramid, scanning the vicinity for any sign of a threat.

She moved from the sheltering structure, away from the majority of people she could see, and skirted around the pyramid grounds, far from the angry mob. Giving a wide berth to a shadowy figure in a soldier's hat who stood frozen, gawking at the quarrel, Violet moved slowly—step and freeze, step and freeze—hoping each movement would attract no attention. She knew she could not become invisible. The bright moon that allowed her to move freely also revealed her in sharp relief against the pale sand.

Hours seemed to pass as she crept away from the pyramid to the dune Leontios had instructed her to shelter behind. To her right, a soft sound resembled a footstep. Violet froze. Slowly, she turned her head, but she could not see anything. All the figures scattered around the ancient site had crept forward, clearly enjoying the drama playing out in the foreground.

"For the last time, move!" an authoritative voice bellowed.

"You don't own this site," another responded. "You clear off."

"Not happening, mate," the first voice yelled. "We've been given charge of protecting the antiquities, and you don't have any right to be here."

"And I say again, I don't need your permission."

A loud sound echoed across the flat landscape. It sounded like flesh hitting flesh.

Someone got punched, Violet realized.

All the lingering figures raced forward, eager to view the fight from closer proximity. Seeing her opportunity, Violet rushed forward with them, her head bent low to hide her feminine features.

At the last moment, she veered away. *Don't see me,* she urged. *Don't notice. See the fight? So much drama. Don't see me. Moon, why must you be so bright.*

A blast of hot wind assaulted her face, and the night grew dark. Almost too dark to see. Violet gulped and looked upward to see a fat cloud scurrying across the surface of the moon. It wasn't particularly large and would only last a moment, but if she hurried…

Her ears strained to take in any warning shouts as she dashed across the open area between the pyramid and the dune, but there was nothing.

She slipped into the darker-than-dark shadow of the towering pile of sand, ducking around the back, farthest from the mêlée and sank to her knees. The cloud passed, allowing light to illuminate Violet's face as she let the satchel on her arm slide to the ground. The contents clunked against each other, and the lantern released a soft, metallic hum as it landed. She lowered her face to the book. *How can it be? How? This isn't possible.*

Long minutes passed as she wept in confused disbelief. *Leave it to you, Violet, to fall for a book. I mean, what could possibly make more sense than that?* The ironic thought broke through her daze, and she had to suppress a bark of hysterical laughter.

Much as I'd like to lie here all night, I can't. I need the man, not the book, to lead me. Hoisting herself to a seat in the sand, she wiped her eyes. She settled the book that somehow was more than even she could ever have realized onto her lap and, opening the cover, she traced the symbols with her fingertip. Their meaning had been burned into her memory. "Me within you," she breathed, her eyes sliding closed. "You within me. By the power of moon and

159

sun, all things—through us—can be done. Come back to me, Leontios. Come back, I need you."

Nothing happened for a long moment as her hand caressed the leather. Under her fingers, the cover stretched out wider and wider. The weight in her lap grew heavier. A familiar touch captured her palm and fingertips.

"We need to hurry," she whispered, not opening her eyes. "A fight has broken out. It's a perfect opportunity to put some distance between us and the pyramid.

Without a word, Leontios laced his fingers through hers and helped her to her feet. The weight of his satchel lifted from her shoulder, and she wriggled it out from around her arm.

"Are you well, VioletWarren?" he asked, his voice concerned.

She shook her head. "Not in the slightest."

"Well, we must move on. Perhaps, when we are far from this place, we can discuss it. For now, please open your eyes and let us go forward."

Her eyelids felt like lead weights. They fought to remain closed, to prevent the final blow to her sense of reality. Yet open they must, and as she knew she would, she jolted at the sight of Leontios's handsome, tattooed face. Her breath shuddered as she inhaled. Yet she let Leontios lead her out into the desert. The sand crunched under her feet, level and bare. The hand in hers felt warm as life itself. Much warmer than the night air, which had grown rather cool after sunset.

The further they got from the pyramid, the wilder the desert became. Small, tough plants clustered in the shade of sand dunes. Lizard tracks and camel prints dotted the sand, the forms illuminated by the glowing moon.

The couple walked in silence for long minutes as they put space between themselves and civilization.

They approached another large dune.

In the shadow of the sandy pile, two men stood facing each other, staring with single-minded intensity. One, younger and shorter, clutched the other by the shoulder. The older, taller man stood statue-still.

Then, the older man moved, darting out serpent fast to crush the younger man's chin in his hand and capture his mouth in a wild kiss.

Violet stepped back again, drawing Leontios away from the couple. Skirting along the far side of the dune, away from the lovers, she muttered, "And I thought my attraction to foreign men was a problem."

"VioletWarren," Leontios said softly as they trekked away again, "what did you see? I thought the men were going to fight."

She shook her head. "They were kissing. I wanted to give them space."

"I do not know what that means," Leontios said.

Violet stopped dead. "Are you serious?"

"Yes," he replied. "This surprises you?"

"Yes! Leontios, a kiss is an almost universal sign of affection. Parents kiss their children. Friends will sometimes greet each other with a kiss, but the kiss between lovers is the most important and passionate of all. How on earth do your people show affection for their lovers without a kiss? How do they prepare for intimacy?" Her cheeks heated at how she blurted out the indiscreet question.

"There are many touches used to show affection. We embrace friends and family members. The special touch between lovers involves the man laying his hand on the woman's, palm to palm. It gives her the option to accept the touch by folding their hands together or rejecting it by pulling away."

"But no kiss?"

He shook his head.

She blinked. "Goodness. I had no idea. Even the Egyptians kissed, though that may have been later, as their empire lasted for many centuries."

"So, you have explained what this… kiss… is for, VioletWarren, but not what it is. What is this magical touch that the whole world has adopted while I was insensible?"

She felt the warmth in her cheeks increasing. "Didn't you see them?"

"I did not understand what I was seeing before

162

you dragged me away," he explained, amusement creasing his mouth and crinkling his eyes.

"A kiss is a touch from one person's lips to a part of the human body. In particular, kisses on the cheek or the top of the head are common between parents and children, or between friends. A man in the early stage of courtship might kiss the back of a woman's hand. When people are committed in a relationship, they will kiss each other on the lips, which both shows love and arouses passion."

"Ah." Leontios seemed to ponder the information. "And in this age, this is a universal signal of romantic affection?"

She nodded.

"So those men were lovers?"

She nodded. "It looks that way."

"Then we should keep moving away from them and give them privacy?"

"I think that would be a good idea. We need to get moving anyway. Which way should we go?"

"This way." Leontios set off. Violet had long since lost track of north, south, east and west after circling so many sand dunes, but her companion moved with such confidence, she had no reason to doubt his conviction.

So, off they went like a pair of maniacs, walking away from every possible help into the wilderness. The flat sand dotted with dunes slowly transformed into a rockier landscape. As they walked, Violet pondered the conversation. *He didn't kiss me because he didn't know how. Not because he didn't want to. I wonder if he would want to…*

She noticed their joined hands. *He laid his palm on mine multiple times and waited. When I didn't respond, he looked disappointed. When I took his hand, he looked confused. That suggests he's attracted to me.* Her stomach thrilled at the realization. *We do desire each other, but we aren't speaking the same touch language.* Her breath caught again.

Well, everything is bizarre, I guess. I met a man yesterday, and I already want to love him. Madly. And… he's a ghost who's been trapped inside a book for several millennia. And I'm not dreaming. She shook her head. *I wanted an adventure, but this isn't exactly what I had in mind. How in the world can I be with a book—provided that really is what he wants. Even if he remains in human form, his culture is entirely foreign to mine.*

And yet, her soul knew him. Knew him and coveted every moment they could spend together. Starting this night on their +journey to nowhere.

CHAPTER 11

A brilliant sunrise chased past the horizon, heating the desert.

Leontios uttered a word Violet didn't understand but felt fairly sure was a curse. "We must abandon our search for today," he said at length. "It will soon be too hot to move safely."

"Have you seen anything you recognize?" Violet asked.

"Several somethings," he replied, "At least, I think I did. Over four thousand years of erosion have altered the landmarks tremendously. I saw a red rock. I remember a red rock. It is much smaller now, as I would have expected, but the shape has changed, so I cannot be sure it was the same one. I have seen several landmarks that might have been familiar but might not have been."

"That's frustrating," Violet agreed, "but we knew this part would not be fast or easy. At least we can tell by the position of the sun that we're facing in the right direction. We are, aren't we?" A blistering ray touched the side of her forehead, and a bead of sweat rolled down her face. "I see some palm trees ahead. Shall we investigate? They don't provide the best shade, but maybe there's more to see there."

Leontios nodded absently.

They crested a sandy hill. Below them, a small oasis surrounded a muddy pool. Two ragged date palms crossed their trunks and hung their foliage low. But best of all, on the far side of the pool, a slanted rock provided a small patch of shade that would last through the hottest part of the day. "That's perfect."

"We are close to our goal," Leontios said solemnly. "This oasis was once a small town affiliated with Skeon. It was much larger then, naturally."

"How do you know?" Violet asked.

Leontios waved to a range of large, rocky hills. "While the size has changed, there is a pattern of faces in the caves below the peaks. They have not changed enough to be unrecognizable."

"But then, where is the city?"

He shrugged. "We are within an hour's walk."

"Only an hour? We should press on then," Violet suggested.

"But I still do not know exactly where the city is in relation to this spring, nor do I know how easy it will be to find. I do not wish to walk an hour to get to the vicinity of Skeon and then spend another several hours wandering around in the sun. We should shelter here and wait until nightfall. Do you think you can sleep, Violet?"

She smiled. "I imagine I can. I feel like I've been walking for a month. Can you believe we've only been on this adventure for a few days?"

He said nothing in response to her inane comment. They scrambled down the hill to the pond, skirted the small pool and crawled into the shadow of the rock. Violet rolled onto her belly and propped herself up on her elbows, setting her bag in front of her and digging into its depths to withdraw a fresh pita bread, split and filled with spicy, roasted meat and strong, smelly cheese. She unwrapped it from its newspaper holder and took a bite while she dug for her water flask.

"Do you think the water in the spring is safe to drink?" she asked, "Or would it be better to conjure it from the air?"

"I believe so," he replied, similarly drawing out his sandwich and imitating her movements. "It was at one time. I do recommend we take the water from the spring itself. The pool is rather unattractive."

"Couldn't you draw water from the air?" she suggested. "You did it once."

"It is more difficult in the deep desert," he explained. "Where we were earlier, there was more moisture in the air. I could, but I do not wish to. Not when this spring is available. It will be easier at night when you can channel the moon."

"I don't know how to do that. So, spring water it is." She rolled onto her side, tired but not yet ready to sleep. "Um, Leontios?"

He turned her way, and she could see from the look on his face that he was far from sure about cheese.

"Assuming we find the way in, what is involved in the ritual to join the crystal? I imagine it's quite *involved*. Is it written on the pages of… well… you?"

"Yes," he agreed. "The description is here." He laid his hand on his ribcage, "but without the context of many years living in Skeon, your ability to translate it into your language will not truly show you the secrets. Those are just my notes."

"The shorthand version?"

He looked at her.

"Never mind. It would take forever to explain, and it's not that interesting. So, Leontios, High Priest of the Sun, brother of the Prince of Skeon, what is involved in draining the crystal so it doesn't erupt?"

"We must work as one, VioletWarren. That is not a metaphor. We must be as one literal person, with the power of sun and moon flowing through us both."

"That will be challenging for me," she pointed out dryly. "I like the moon and all, but I don't know how to let her power *flow* through me."

"I will help you enter a receptive state," he promised. "There is, as you surmised, a ritual to prepare us. Once we are prepared, the draining is simple enough. There is a pool with a spring. In my time, it was much bigger and prettier than this one. A true desert oasis in the cleft of the rock. We join hands. You touch the water. I touch the crystal, and the magic flows through us into the water, where it dissipates into the surrounding soil and plants."

"Sounds simple. Does it hurt?"

"I suspect it will. Normally, it feels like a gentle tingle, but normally it is drained once each month."

"Ouch," Violet commented. She took another bite of her overripe sandwich and swished some water in her mouth, swallowing it down. "Um, Leo, are you sure we can survive that?"

"Sadly, no," he replied. "It may be too much for our bodies to sustain."

She frowned.

"But if all goes well, the power should not do us

lasting harm. It is meant to flow. My worry is mostly that you will fight it. That could be deadly. Are you good at submitting?"

Violet scoffed and tucked the sandwich away in her bag. "Not at all."

"That is what I feared. It is a lovely quality, but perhaps not the best for this mission. Will you try?"

She sighed. "I'm only just now accepting that this is all real. I'm still deciding whether hysterics would be a more fitting response."

"Fair."

She rolled onto her back and sat up. "So, tell me more. You know I adore antiquities, and we have many hours to pass. Many more than I need or will be able to sleep. What do I need to do to prepare myself to be a conduit of energy for a magic I don't quite believe exists?"

His lips curved upward, but the sadness that scrunched the corners of his eyes spoke volumes. "First, we must anoint our bodies in oil."

"Do you have some?"

"I do," he replied. "It was abundant and inexpensive at the market once I understood how the… money? How the money worked. I purchased it while you were selecting foods. Ellani always hated the oil."

"Who's Ellani?" Violet interrupted.

"My wife," Leontios replied, his attention still

focused on his sandwich. He curled his lip in an undeniable sneer.

Violet shot to her feet, banging her head against the rock under which they sheltered. She sat down hard. "You're married?"

"Yes. Of course. Without my high priestess of the moon, I could not perform the rituals, as I said."

Violet bit her lip. "I didn't realize. I'm sorry."

"For what, VioletWarren?"

She closed her eyes, not sure how to explain.

Leontios pulled her closer to him, rubbing the top of her head to soothe the sting of the impact. "Are you well?"

She closed her eyes, tears stinging with the pain of body and heart.

For the first time in their brief acquaintance, Leontios embraced her, aligning their bodies as close as possible while sitting side by side. "Please, talk to me, Violet," he urged. "Why are you upset?"

"Leontios, you're married. You have a wife. I think…" she sucked in a lung full of air and released it in a slow hiss. "I thought there was something more between us. I mean, the lovers' touch is this, right?" She grasped his hand and let their fingers slide together.

"Yes." He looked confused. "Why?"

Think, Violet. Why? "I recall you said that marriage was rare in your society, yes?" She pulled back from the embrace and looked into his eyes.

"Yes." He still looked puzzled, and no wonder.

How can he understand if you don't explain? Yet what words could convey this in a way he would understand? "Perhaps, like the concept of kissing, it's a difference in understanding. In this time, marriage is both common and extremely important. It's a political, religious and personal vow to honor their bond and never become intimate with another person, as long as they both shall live."

Leontios raised an eyebrow. "It is different," he explained. "Yes, marriage refers to a political and religious commitment, but it is not a personal vow. Even the tiny number of people who are married are welcome to seek love elsewhere. It is a ceremonial connection which can be personal but does not need to be."

"Oh," Violet breathed. "I think I understand. So Ellani was your ceremonial wife, which means she performed rituals with you?"

He nodded.

"But you didn't love her?"

"No, Violet. I did love her. I loved her with all I had in me."

She bit her lip, eyes stinging.

"She did not love me. She had a mate, which is a separate thing, a personal commitment anyone and everyone is likely to make."

"I'm sorry." She laid a hand on his arm. "That

must have hurt. But, Leo, if you love your wife, why are you touching my hand like a lover?"

He sighed. "It is difficult to explain. You have seen already how we have struggled to communicate."

"You are quite right about that," she concurred, "but won't you try anyway?"

"I will try. Will you try to understand?" he asked, watching her closely.

She nodded.

"I have loved Ellani for years, but for her, our marriage was always more political than personal. I believe she cared about me, but her heart belonged to Kel. Up until I woke up after my thousands of years as a book, she was the person I most felt drawn to, but I always knew I did not mean to her what she meant to me."

"I suppose, also, that though she's been gone a long time, she must feel like she's still with you."

"She was killed the day Egypt sacked Skeon. Shot through with an arrow. I placed her soul inside the key the way I placed mine inside the book. So, she is here in the world somehow, maybe. Like Skeon itself, the key is fragile and prone to destruction, but at the moment, my options were limited."

"You did the best you could for her," Violet reassured him. "All this does not reassure me, though. She sounds like the love of your life."

"She was."

"And now?"

"Now… and then, Violet. Now and then, I knew that if I wanted to love and be loved, I would need to be open to someone else—as she was—because she was not for me. I could not will it to happen." To punctuate the point, he laid his hand against her palm again.

Violet gulped, understanding but not quite believing his message. Unable to cope, she pulled away, rejecting the touch. Dropping her lumpy, uncomfortable satchel on the sand, she lay down and used it to pillow her head.

Though she doubted she'd be able to rest on such a worthless support, with so many objects digging into her face, with sand seeping into her clothing, and the rising heat drawing sweat to the surface of her skin, she dropped off instantly.

In her sleep, the crystal loomed before her again, white and covered in sharp protuberances. It was beautiful and dangerous.

She felt a presence behind her and knew without turning that it was Leontios. "Is this our goal then?"

He wrapped his arms around her waist and rested his chin on her shoulder. "It is. I love her as much as I hate her."

Somehow, she knew he meant the crystal—and more.

"We must be careful, VioletWarren. There is

much more against us than just what we think. If we can even get to this, it will be a miracle."

"What's against us?" she asked.

"You will know when the time is right," his voice murmured in her ear. "Be yourself in all your wild ambition, your adventurous spirit, your open heart. Love and courage, Violet. Love and courage."

A gun roared in her dream, and Violet woke with a start.

The angle of the sun against the rock cast a long shadow.

In sleep, as when awake, Violet had drawn close to Leontios. In fact, her head rested on his shoulder. His arm encircled her. They breathed in tandem. Their pulses throbbed together.

I've known this man less than a week. Somehow, that didn't matter.

He's from a very different time and place. That also didn't matter.

He's a book. She braced one arm on his chest and leaned over him, examining his face. In sleep—*how does a book sleep?* —his face had relaxed, mouth sagged to release a soft snore. Leontios looked even more beautiful and compelling than he did when awake.

How can I feel so much so fast? She no longer cared to think through the rational realities of relationships. Not when she lay so close to this man, inhaling his scent, which she now realized smelled not only like an old book but like *her* old book. *He's been with me so long. Years. Most of my adult life.*

His dark eyes fluttered open, and he stared up into hers. His intense expression spoke of powerful thoughts he did not utter.

Again, his hand sought hers, though this time he looked sadder and more tentative than in the previous times they'd touched. *I rejected him,* she remembered. *Just before I fell asleep. Just after he told me how his wife had rejected him for another man throughout their entire marriage. She died thousands of years ago that felt like less than a week in his awareness. And he still dared reach out to me.*

She swallowed hard and laced her fingers through his again, accepting that though they had many more discussions before they could truly say they understood each other, this connection transcended understanding.

The touch warmed her beyond the heat of one sweaty palm in another. As her guard lowered, her spirit seemed to slip beyond the bounds of her body and mingle with his so that their joined hands created a new singularity. A new being. One made of magic and modernity, knowledge and wisdom, life and that which is beyond this life. Though all of it contradicted, it still made perfect sense.

Leaning forward, Violet brought her face down close to Leontios's. She slid her eyes closed and kissed him.

Leontios's lips felt firm and soft at the same time. Throughout her thirty years, Violet had allowed more than one gentleman to kiss her, but never had it felt like this. So right. So *perfect*. As though their lips had been made specifically to fit each other like a key in a lock. *The way our hands fit. The way our souls fit.* No man would ever belong to her the way this one did, and she felt a peace she could never explain rise up in her. *No explanation will ever be as satisfying as just letting this be. It's fate.*

She lifted her head.

"That was delightful," he breathed. "I understand how such a touch became so popular."

She smiled. "I don't know why you trust me," she said, "but I appreciate it."

Unlike his previous wry half-grins, this time, his teeth flashed, and his eyes sparkled. He said nothing, but his expression spoke words that did not exist in either of their languages.

His free hand slid up her back and tucked into her hair, urging her back down.

"More?" she teased, eyes wide with teasing false innocence.

"Please," he begged.

Violet succumbed instantly, compressing his lips with her own, which remained slightly parted so she could tempt him with a gentle jab of her tongue. *I always hated this,* she recalled, *and it always felt disgusting until now. Now, nothing matters more than being as close to this man as I can possibly be.*

Smart man that he was, Leontios asked no questions. He simply let her guide the kiss, opening to receive the touch and even responding with a gentle glide. No aggressive stabs of his tongue into her mouth, just an eager, easy exploration that left her panting with arousal. Her breasts and belly tingled.

As though he had known his whole life how kisses led to more, Leontios rolled, covering her body with his, so his firm, full sex compressed her abdomen.

"Oh, God," Violet breathed. "Oh, Leontios, what is happening?"

"Very good things," he reminded her. "Things worth risking everything to save."

Violet sighed, their strange reality invading the embrace, along with a vague sense of unease. *It's not safe here,* a tiny thread of intuition warned her. *Something is looking for you, and this is too good a place to look.*

Violet cleared her throat, passion fading. "Which means we should probably delay this exploration until we've saved it. It won't do us any good to fall into each other's arms and let the disaster overtake us. Not when we have the chance to set everything to rights. After, we will have all the time in the world to make this…" she indicated their joined hands, "everything we ever dreamed."

He grinned, but his eyes looked sad. "Too wise. How could I forget." With a sigh, he hauled himself to his feet and, by tugging gently on her fingers, helped her to emerge from beneath their sheltering rock.

Though a little shattered at how abruptly the tender interlude had ended, she recognized that the low sun meant it was time for them to start moving. *If Leontios really is a book—which he is—does that mean the rest of the mission is also real? Are we really going to find a hidden city out here in the middle of nowhere, a city with a giant, overflowing crystal we need to use magic to diffuse? What a strange concept.*

Still not sure what to make of any part of the situation, she dragged her bottle out of the satchel and made her way around their shelter to the active side of the spring, where water bubbled up from the earth, clear and clean, before gathering in a muddy pool that quickly drained back into the sand. She knelt in the dampness, moistening the knees of her trousers as she dipped the bottle into the water.

Meanwhile, the sound of rustling paper told her Leontios was attempting to eat the pita again. "I do not care for this," he admitted.

"I don't either," she replied, "but the salt will help us keep our bodies in balance. Too much sweat and too much water can be dangerous. Wait, you're from the desert. You must know this better than I do."

"I suppose so," he agreed. "Are the other foods more palatable than this?"

"I think so," she agreed. "I have dates, plain pitas and chickpea balls. You have olives and dried sausages that smell like goat, but no more cheese. Better finish it. We don't have much to spare, and age won't improve it."

He sighed again.

Violet finished filling her canteen and took her own advice, chewing the unpalatable sandwich in hopes of making it disappear as quickly as possible. Leontios took her position at the spring, filling his vessel—an old-fashioned skin bag.

"What direction must we go?" Violet asked.

"Southwest. Always southwest," Leontios replied. He pulled a hat over his head—where it clashed with his otherworldly appearance—and turned to face the open desert. The sunset's brilliant red orb beamed uncomfortably into Violet's eyes as she stared after him. Plopping her own much more fashionable hat onto her head, she hurried after him.

Despite the sun slowly sinking toward the horizon, the heat remained intense. Sweat immediately sprang up on her skin.

She caught up and slowed to a sedate pace that better preserved her strength. "It's fortunate for you," she pointed out, "that I'm athletic and adventurous."

Leontios did not respond. Nor did he reach out to take her hand as he normally did. They trudged along in uncomfortable silence as the sun slipped lower and lower until it finally disappeared. Steps became miles as the couple searched for something one did not understand and the other could not find. As the hours passed, the latter fact became more and more evident.

Finally, he sank to a seat in the sand at the base of a towering rock formation—one of many. Angry words Violet couldn't understand but suspected were curses spilled from him.

"No luck?" she guessed.

He shook his head. "After so many years, most of the formations have changed shape drastically. Even with the key, I would struggle to find what I'm looking for."

She sank to a seat beside him. He still made no move to touch her. The loss of their easy intimacy made her sad.

"Are you angry with me?" she asked.

He shook his head. Though the moon was less full this night, it provided plenty of light for her to see his movements. "Not angry, no. Thinking about Ellani made me sad. Also, there are some differences between your time and mine that are causing us not to communicate clearly."

"I agree," Violet said. "We can overcome them if we try. I'm sure you must be very sad about remembering your wife, though. Do you want to talk about her?" She laid a hand on his shoulder.

"Why?" he asked, looking over his shoulder to fix her with his compelling dark eyes.

"It just occurred to me that, while all the sadness you experienced took place over four thousand years ago, it must feel to you like it happened last week. I think, if a person lost their spouse and watched their city burn at the same time, they'd be quite sad a week later."

"Yes, it is sad," he agreed, drawing in a ragged breath. "I am hoping that by doing this work, I can either assuage the grief or…"

"Or just have a reason to keep going?"

He nodded.

His pain flared bright in his dark gaze. Violet could feel it stabbing into her own heart. She shimmied around him and plunked sideways into his lap, lacing her fingers into his hair, knocking his hat into the sand and drawing his lips down to hers. She kissed him in empathy. In attraction. In commiseration. *In caring,* she realized. *It would be so easy to fall in love. I've never felt anything like this before.*

She clung to him, hoping her touch and presence would bring him some comfort.

Leontios's arms snaked around her, and he crushed her to his chest.

She nestled into his warmth, giving solace and taking their connection deeper into herself. *How could anyone* not *love this man?* she wondered. *I barely met him, and he's already essential to my future.* She recalled all the males in the past who had tried to possess her. Not one had touched her heart. Leontios, in only a few days, had taken up residence there.

"We should keep trying," he said at last, scrubbing the side of his hand along his nose. "It may be unlikely that we will achieve our goal, but if we do not try, we are sure to fail." He helped Violet to her feet, retrieved his hat and stuffed it into his satchel. "I will observe the formations while keeping in mind how the pyramid changed with the centuries. That surely must help."

"How is the city concealed?" Violet asked. "How can an entire oasis be hidden?"

"There is a wall of stone behind—containing the cave that was once the royal palace—as well as to the front and all sides. The way into the oasis is narrow. I have rendered it invisible against the rest of the rocks."

"But there is no gate?"

"No gate," he agreed. "We did not need one. Unless you know the way, the door is hidden. At least, it is now. In its heyday, Skeon spilled beyond the valley into the desert. We carried water out from the spring to water crops and animals. A stone path led to the door like an arrow."

"Might we not find the path, then?" Violet suggested.

"I destroyed it," he replied. "Our crystal is life itself. I could not allow our enemies to take it. I obliterated the entire outer city down to bare earth. I have no doubt the sand has reclaimed it all by now. In all honesty, I did not expect to be released, so I did not consider the complications of trying to find the city thousands of years later and without the key."

He paused, scanning the rocks for any signs of irregularity.

"If there's no gate, then how can there be a key? What is it?" Violet also stared hard at the glowing white rock. Gentle moonlight made it possible to look. In the sun, it would have been blinding.

"A small piece taken from the larger crystal. It is a smooth white stone about the size of my palm, shaped into the trident symbol of the prince of Skeon. When you look through it, it is easier to see the subtle changes in color that mark the opening."

"A refractor," Violet breathed. "That makes sense. Breaking the light into different colors will diffuse the blinding effect and reveal hidden pockets."

"I do not know what 'refractor' means, but essentially, yes. What you are saying sounds true. The key changes the way we see the landscape. It makes the invisible visible."

"Then wouldn't any crystal likely do the same?" she demanded.

Leontios turned to her, lowering his eyebrows in concentration. "Perhaps. I saw the key's work as magical. The connection between the large and small pieces would draw our eye to the correct place, but… if it is a phenomenon you have discovered in this current age…" he paused, regarding her closely. "Perhaps. Should we then return to Memphis—er, Cairo? There were many jewel shops. Perhaps one could supply us with what we need."

"I don't think that will be necessary," she replied, digging into her bag. "I bought this quite a while ago, back in Pittsburgh. I don't know why I felt the need to bring it to Egypt, but, like the book, I don't like to be parted from it. And it sounds very similar to your key, so maybe it will work almost as well?" She dug into her back and drew out the clear quartz crystal.

Leontios stared. Long minutes passed while he gawked in awe at the small object. Then he gulped, and when he spoke, his voice sounded ragged. "This is it, VioletWarren. This is the key. How by all the heavens did you come to have it?"

"I don't know," she replied, stunned to discover that the silly indulgence she couldn't stop herself from buying had turned out to be so important.

"Perhaps the moon herself brought it to you. Perhaps you were meant for this journey."

"That's what the fortune teller who sold it to me said. I mean, more or less. She didn't describe this exactly, but she did say I would journey across the sea and meet a mysterious stranger." She gulped. "What does it all mean?"

"It means that you were born to be my priestess. Come, my darling Violet. Let us use this key to reveal the door. I will soon be able to show you my home."

Leontios lifted the crystal, but the dim moonlight did not possess enough strength to cast any rainbows.

"Shall we wait until sunrise?" she asked.

He shook his head. "It is too dangerous. It may still take several hours to locate the door, and we cannot be out in the sun so long. The warm night tells me the day will be even hotter than those before. Can you light your lantern? See if we can make this flash in the dark?"

It took Violet's trembling fingers a ridiculous amount of time to unlatch the buckle of her satchel and remove their scarcely used lantern. She struggled to work the mechanism on the glass box.

Leontios grasped Violet's wrist. "Let us move away from this place," he suggested.

Violet froze. "Did you see something?" Visions

of British soldiers, of Egyptian Nationals, of unknown gunmen loomed in her mind.

"It is not what I see but what I feel," he explained. "Though the threat has not yet found us, it is looking. It will come. We must be gone before it does. In darkness is better."

"What is it?" she asked, more nervous than ever.

He shook his head. "I cannot say. Not for certain. Come with me. Let us move on by moonlight and light your lantern when we are away." He took her hand and led her away to the south, following the cliff face. Long minutes passed as they made their way away from whatever threat Leontios had perceived. *I felt it too,* she recalled. *In the oasis before we set out. Can I feel it now? Maybe.*

The moonlight reflected on the white sand and the white stone. A pair of jackals began squealing to each other, one in the near distance, the other much further away. Their high-pitched cries sent a chill up Violet's spine.

Leontios pulled her closer, wrapping his arm around her waist.

"Leontios," Violet breathed, "are you seeing any landmarks as we move?"

"It is too dark," he replied, "and so much has changed. So much."

"Then let's stop and look. We don't want to get too far away from our oasis in case we can't find the door tonight."

Leontios paused in his forward rush. "I do not feel safe here. The threat remains, and yet… Perhaps it will be impossible to escape."

His words chilled her.

"Very well, VioletWarren. Light your lantern. When you do, call up the clouds. Let us concentrate the light through the key so we can better see its magic."

Though she was still not entirely sure she possessed this power, Violet thought hard about moisture. There wasn't much, only a trace, but she thought about it, nonetheless. Thought about it drawing together into three billowing puffs and placing them between the moon and them.

The silver light dimmed. Violet opened eyes she couldn't remember closing. Three thin wisps concealed the brightest light. Shivering in a warm breeze, Violet operated the mechanism to light the lantern. A pale light shot out, part of it directly onto the white-faced cliff before them. "Will this work?" she breathed, barely making a sound.

"This is perfect," he murmured, his warm breath caressing her ear.

A different kind of shiver ran down Violet's spine. It spawned a riot of butterflies in her belly. Uncomfortable with her arousal, she dug the crystal out of her bag and handed it to Leontios. He extended it into the beam of light, and a rainbow shot forward, painting the rock with color.

Somehow, the refraction brought the hollows and depressions in the rock into sharper relief. The darkness no longer concealed the cliff's secrets.

No magical gate appeared to their gaze, but Violet could immediately see how the key would work. "Very interesting," she commented. "Shall we go north or further south?"

"South," he replied. "I do not know why, but north seems unsafe."

She didn't point out that if they remained exposed to the elements in daylight, they would be in more danger than from some undefined threat. After all, he had been taking them south all along. South seemed the right way to go.

They moved along the cliff face, shining the light on the rocks and examining the depressions for anything that seemed more significant than a mere alcove, but no sign of a gateway appeared. An hour of scrutiny yielded no results.

"Leontios," Violet said gently, "We should return to the oasis. It's a long walk, and the night is waning."

He snorted in frustration. "You are correct," he said. "I hate to admit it, but we dare not risk our safety."

Reluctantly, they turned back to the north.

To distract him from their mutual disappointment, she made quiet conversation as she tucked the crystal away in her bag. "So, we got—errrr—

sidetracked earlier when you were describing the ritual to me. I recall you saying we would anoint our bodies in oil. What happens next?"

"Next, we invoke the sun and moon," he explained, his attention focused on the rock face beside them as he hunted for clues. "Throughout the night, we chant and merge our energies so that, at the moment the sun breaches the horizon, we can act as one."

"Interesting," Violet commented. "What does it mean to merge energies? Is that another ritual?" She glanced at Leontios and saw his grin.

"Not strictly a ritual, no," he replied. "In fact, merging energies is most simply accomplished by intercourse, though chanting through it is advisable. When engaged in such enjoyable activities, it is easy to become distracted."

Violet froze, the lantern slipping through her fingers to land on the sand with a soft thud. "What?"

Leontios turned to her. "What is wrong, Violet-Warren? Is chanting during intercourse no longer common?"

Violet gulped as she retrieved the lantern and switched it off. "Um, Leo, ritual sex is no longer common." Her face burned at the frank admission. "Physical intimacy is considered highly private."

"Well, of course, such things are private. Not all rituals are meant for the public eye. But I am puzzled. How can you invoke fertility rites without intercourse?"

Violet felt quite sure her face would soon catch fire. "Um, we don't go in much for fertility rites. Our religion is more… symbolic."

"By all the heavens. Are you certain? No, of course you are. But I do not understand. How can your people reproduce without intercourse?"

"It exists," she admitted. "Of course, people still make love. As you say, it's how more people come to be. It's just… Only married people are supposed to do it. As I mentioned, marriage is not as restricted for us as it was for you. Nearly everyone gets married eventually."

"Yes, this I can imagine. But let us keep moving." He applied gentle pressure on her back.

Violet allowed herself to be directed. "Um, so I want to be sure I understand your perspective. As you said earlier, for your people, marriage was a religious and political rite reserved for high priests and royalty?"

"Correct." A gentle press on her shoulder urged her back closer to the cliff. "Let us stay close to the rocks. Perhaps we will be less visible in the shadow."

"Perhaps," she agreed, "and to clarify, common people do bond into families, but there is no ritual to seal the bond?"

"Also correct," Leontios agreed.

"Then what happens," she continued, "when people decide they don't want to be together anymore? How did you stop families from being broken?" She glanced at his face.

He looked puzzled but did not answer.

"Keeping families together is not a priority?" His frown didn't change. "Who is responsible for the care of the children then?"

"Everyone," he replied. "Children are the future. Everyone is responsible for their care. As for whom they live with, it depends. A suckling babe obviously stays with its mother. An older child would move around. And keep in mind that extended families lived in sort of compounds, so mother and father never would have been the only options. None of this is true anymore, is it?"

Violet shook her head. "In some cases, grandparents, other relatives or godparents will take in an orphan or a widowed mother and child, but most of the time people expect the husband to provide for the family and the woman to tend the home and children."

Leontios shook his head. "I think that it will take more than one night to understand these different views. What we must determine is how this will affect the ritual. I feel that you are trying to distract yourself from something important you must address, and I think I can guess. In a society where sexual relations mean something very different, it bothers you to use them for this utilitarian purpose. Is that correct?"

"Somewhat," Violet admitted, "though that barely begins to encompass the problem. Leontios, I'm a virgin."

He paused in walking again. "I do not know what that means," he admitted, "though it seems very important to you. Please explain."

Violet licked her lips. "I have never had relations with any man. In this time, it is expected that women will remain... untouched until marriage."

"Truly?" Leontios's puzzled expression tightened down until his eyebrows touched, and the crinkles around his eyes and mouth seemed to glow in the moonlight. "Is such a thing even possible? How do your authorities enforce it?"

She shook her head. "No one enforces it, but a woman who is intimate with men before marriage loses her reputation."

"But if sexual relations are so private, as you say, how does anyone know?"

"Gossip," she replied simply. "Also, a man expects his wife to be a virgin on their wedding night. And therein lies the problem. I don't plan to marry, Leontios, but I haven't ruled it out. I'm already odd and old. If I also wasn't a virgin, I might lose my last bargaining chip."

"I do not know what a chip is," Leontios told

her, "but if a man does not value you without these bargains, he does not deserve you."

The butterflies fluttered in her stomach.

"Still, if you feel strongly by the rules of your people that you cannot lie with me, we will have to try another method to help us work as one."

"Thank you," she said quietly, feeling both relieved and strangely deflated. "Aren't we going a bit far, though?"

"What do you mean?" he demanded.

"I think I saw the place we turned south at the cliff face about twenty paces back."

Leontios said a word that she didn't understand but felt was probably a curse. "You are right. This does not look famil—" He stopped, his words dying.

"What?" Violet demanded.

"Do you see this large red rock?

Violet nodded. It was hard to miss. It stood so tall and so different from the surrounding white stones.

"I believe it is what we used to call The Sentinel. Of course, the symbols are long gone, but something about the shape and especially the color makes me wonder."

"How far from the gate is The Sentinel?" Violet asked. Excitement began to bubble in her belly.

"Perhaps an hour. Perhaps less. It will depend as

always on whether I can identify the door in the dark, key or no."

Violet pondered this information. "Should we press on to the north then? Or shall we return to the oasis? If we find the gate, will there be shelter within?"

"Yes," he said. "Remember that I told you there was a cave that was once the royal palace and throne room? It will prevent the sun from reaching us, and as it is also the location from which the spring emerges to fill the pool, it is—or was—lined with soft, soft moss. Soft as any bed. If we find it, we should sleep in comfort."

Yelping barks split the night as the jackals prowled. A thick cloud rolled across the surface of the moon. A cold born, not of the desert night but of something worse, something malevolent, chased up her spine. "Only a few days into our adventure, and I already long for comfort. What a spoiled city girl I'm turning out to be." She chuckled, but it had a hint of hysteria in it.

"You feel it, do you not, VioletWarren?" Leontios asked, squeezing her hand. "You feel the threat in the air? The further north we go, the more it closes on us. We must move quickly. Not only to escape the dawn."

Violet didn't answer. She felt in some way that naming the threat would draw its attention. Instead, she hurried forward, keeping the glowing white wall of the cliff beside them. *It will be our guide. It will keep us on course.*

Somehow, as each hour passed into the night, it seemed more possible that Skeon was real, that they would find it and all of Leontios's wild stories would be true.

The night deepened. Darkened. The edge of dawn, not present but approaching, brought a breath of lightness. At length, Leontios stopped. "VioletWarren, please, give me the key."

She dug into the satchel and withdrew the chunk of crystal, handing it to her companion. "Do you need the light?" She lifted the unlit lantern.

"I do, thank you." He lifted the key between them as she again illuminated the device. A small pool of light emerged and hit the key, setting rainbows flashing in the night. They shone against the stark white of the cliff face.

Violet squinted, hunting for she knew not what. "Do you see anything?"

He waved his free hand. "Please, we are not alone," he hissed.

Violet whipped her head around, searching the open desert. Anyone approaching from that direction would be visible instantly. She saw nothing.

Leontios grabbed her lantern hand, stabilizing it. "There," he breathed.

She turned to see his finger pointing at the rock where, above their heads, a bright golden bar of light aligned directly with a thick overhang. Below, deep blue stained a narrow notch.

"Is that it?" she whispered.

He nodded. Even in the low light, she could see his Adam's apple move. "Come," he urged, his voice rough.

I can only imagine what he must be feeling. For him, this was a thriving city-state last week. Seeing it must be excruciating.

He lowered the crystal to his side. The vision of the rock and the opening vanished, but Leontios took Violet's hand and led her forward with confidence. They stepped into deeper shadow. Drew close enough to touch the rock. Passed through an opening so narrow it seemed little more than a crack in the stone... except that it wasn't. It angled away from the visible rock in a tunnel that could not be perceived until she entered it. The passage continued on until Violet felt she was entering a mountain. The darkness was intense. It pressed in on her with palpable weight. Only the thin beam of light from the lantern illuminated a few steps before them.

She wanted to ask him how long the tunnel was, but she didn't dare break the breathless silence. Even the clinking of the lantern's ring seemed to be inviting threatening forces to swoop down from the rocky ceiling above them.

Violet's breath caught. Her heart pounded. She felt as though the walls were crowding in on her.

And then, without warning, the tunnel opened. The moonlight revealed an open enclosure the size of three city blocks. Water splashed from a cave opposite the exterior wall into a sparkling pool. Around it, despite the desert sand outside, thick vegetation grew in a wild tangle.

A strange hum seemed to vibrate in their air. Though she couldn't quite hear it with her physical ears, she could feel that it consisted of overlapping, discordant tones. It pulsed, she realized, and it seemed to be coming from behind her. She whirled and caught her breath. Behind her, a massive hunk of quartz the size of a car was partially embedded in the rock wall.

Violet's knees gave way. She sank to a seat on ground that was not composed of sand but rather of soft moss, not just under the overhang, but all around the pool as well as in the shadow of the exterior wall.

"Welcome, VioletWarren, to the inner city of Skeon." Though his pronouncement rang, sonorous in the reverberating space, his words seem to catch and tear at his throat. "If only you could have seen it… Seen it…" his voice broke.

Violet left the lantern and her satchel on the ground and rose on unsteady legs, staggering toward him. "It's beautiful. It's like nothing I could have ever seen or imagined."

He drew close, but unlike all the times they had touched, he hesitated, his tattooed face scrunched into a painful, unreadable expression.

She launched herself against him, wrapping her arms around his torso. "I'm so sorry," she murmured. "I can't imagine what you must be feeling."

His hands came to rest on her back.

Violet leaned her head against his chest, cuddling him as he trembled in her embrace. He sank to a seat as though his legs had lost strength, and she found herself in his lap.

She looked up into his face. The whites of his eyes had reddened, and the deep crinkles in the corners of his eyes and around his mouth had turned harsh and sad.

As though unable to restrain himself, Leontios leaned down, touching his lips to her forehead, eyelids, cheeks and ending up on her mouth. The light touch turned wild. Leontios ate at her lips as though the kiss might bring some end to his intense grief.

Yet, when he lifted his head, his pain remained undimmed.

"You're a fast learner," she quipped stupidly, not so much to comfort him as to break the tension.

Leontios said nothing.

"Um, is the crystal supposed to be making that sound?"

He shook his head. "It always hums," he admitted in a rough, harsh voice, "but not like this. I cannot imagine such pressure. It should have erupted long since." He swallowed hard, squinting at the crystal. "It has sprung a small leak. Can you see the dribble of light running down to the ground from that crack near the bottom?"

Violet looked hard at the crystal and realized she could see the leak. Could see the crack from which a thin trickle of energy meandered downward. "It's not enough, is it? The pressure is still building, and this little relief isn't going to buy us much more time."

"I doubt we have no more than a couple of days. A week at most. We must drain it immediately."

"At the moment of sunrise, isn't it?"

He nodded.

"That's coming soon. What must we do? You said we anoint our bodies with oil. Any specific parts? What else must we do?"

"I do not exactly know," Leontios replied. "I have never attempted this without the ritual intercourse. I have heard that it is possible. An ancestor of mine's high priestess was his twin sister. They did not lie together. But since they shared a womb, they had no trouble acting as one. However, they kept no written record of their method. I only know the traditional method. You must place the oil on the key points of your body: along the top of your head, from the center of your forehead up to the hairline, along your nose down to your bottom lip, a line down the center of your throat, a line across your heart from nipple to nipple, a cross on your belly, one on the bottom of each foot and on the palm of each hand. Then, we hold hands, right to left. I will touch the crystal, and you will kneel to touch the water. The magic will flow through me, through you and into the pool.

Violet bit her lip. "I'm afraid," she admitted. "This sounds like it could go terribly wrong."

"It could," he agreed. "Legend says that if the priest and priestess cannot act as one, the magic will burn them alive."

"Lovely." Violet closed her eyes. "I suppose the risk is greater since the crystal is so pent up."

"That seems likely," he agreed. "To be honest, Violet, I would prefer not to experiment with untried techniques. I understand that you are reluctant to take such a step, but… It would make me more comfortable if we could complete the ritual properly."

Violet considered his request. From his perspective, it made perfect sense. Of course, it did. He'd been married to—and sleeping with—a woman who didn't love him for ritual and religious purposes for a long time. *And be honest with yourself.*

You're tempted. You're insanely attracted to this man you've barely met. Violet sighed. *The reason I can't do it is that it's just a ritual to him. Not love. Not even the beginnings of love—which would already strain decency beyond the breaking point.* She thought of the unknown. Of Leontios's strong, tattooed hands on her body, teasing secret pleasures. Then she thought of the reason he would be doing it. *For magic. For power. Not because we love each other.* "I can't," she wailed.

Leontios frowned. "Very well, VioletWarren. We will do the best we can without. I only hope it is enough." For a moment so brief she could have sworn she'd imagined it, a pain that eclipsed his sorrow over the loss of his entire world flared behind his dark eyes. It made her soul ache.

He lowered his eyelids, blocking her out of his deepest feelings. When he opened them again, it looked as though an iron plate had come up between them. *After all, how much rejection can a man take?* The realization hurt her, but there was no time to work through it. Even in the short minutes they'd been in Skeon, the sound coming from the crystal had changed. Higher in pitch and more discordant, it seemed to scrape at the inside of Violet's skull.

"It will be dawn soon," she pointed out.

"You are correct," he replied, his voice devoid of expression. "Here is the oil. Do not waste it. This may require multiple attempts. Do you remember the directions?"

She nodded and accepted the small flask of oil. "Is there a place where I can apply this in privacy?"

He waved at the rock overhang that led into the cave.

"Does anything live in there?" she asked.

"How should I know?" Leontios replied. "I have not been here in several thousand years. When Skeon was alive, the king and the royal family lived there. It was our palace. It goes back quite far. We divided up the space with textiles. Torches and oil lamps lit the inside. The walls were painted with the richest colors. It was glorious."

She smiled. "I wish I could have seen it."

He crimped his lips. It was not a smile.

Violet scurried into the cave-like structure, suppressing her urge to squeal as several bats zoomed in from a night hunting bugs and took up their places around the ceiling.

Shaking her head, she loosened her clothing and removed her boots. Then she poured a small puddle of oil into her left hand and, with her right index finger, stroked a thin line over the part of her hair, across her forehead, on her throat. She felt deeply unsettled as she reached beneath her clothing to stroke the oil in all the various spots Leontios had mentioned. *He's upset with me, and I don't blame him. I wish I could explain that I'm not avoiding… his ritual because I dislike him. It's because I like him too much. I don't know if he would understand. There's too much cultural context lost.*

Violet's task only took a moment. She emerged from the cave, leaves and dirt sticking to the oil on the soles of her feet, and silently extended the flask to Leontios.

He had used the time to strip off his own clothing so that he stood barefoot and shirtless, the moonlight glowing on his tanned body, his tattoos contrasting darkly. Now, she could see so much more of her beloved book etched on his skin. The symbols and sketches she'd pored over for years tucked into the curves of his arms, chased in lines down his ribs. Each toe bore a symbol, each foot a sentence. His beauty stole her breath.

She gulped.

I wish I were the type of woman to lie down with a man I barely know. Him being himself is reason enough, no ritual needed. But because the ritual was needed —needed more than the strange love that seemed to be growing between them—her heart protested.

I want to be loved, not used. Too many men have tried to use me. If Leontios did as well—not because he wants to curry favor with my father, not because he wants my money, but because some arcane religious rite demands it—I think it might just be the end of me.

A quiet slurping noise indicated that the bottle's stopper had been replaced. Violet raised her eyes to

Leontios, found him watching her watch him. For a moment, the guarded expression lowered again. Lowered to reveal the haunted eyes of a man who had seen too much, done too much, and was no longer sure if he was fit for the human race.

She stepped forward without thought, already in the habit of touching him. Her arms slid around his neck and tugged him down, capturing his lips in a kiss of undeniable passion. "I care for you, Leo. I do," she murmured against his skin. "I care so much. Please be patient with me. Things are different now. It's not because I think badly of you."

He swallowed. "I do not understand, but I do thank you for saying so. It is vital that we connect as best we can."

She nodded, grieving the loss of the open-hearted intimacy that had grown between them.

Brightness began to illuminate the sky behind the rock wall that enclosed the central city of Skeon. With it came a sense, not of rightness or safety, but of risk. "We should… move forward?" she suggested.

"We should." He stepped back from the embrace.

Still hurting from their tense conversation, she reached out and laced her fingers through his, hoping that by using his culture's language of romance, he would understand her conflicted feelings —not to mention her unwavering affection.

He froze, scrutinizing her face. His facial tattoos rolled on a twisted expression of confusion.

I'm sorry, she thought at him. *I never wanted to hurt you.*

He lowered his eyebrows and tugged on their joined hands, leading her toward the crystal, positioning them between it and the pool.

Violet knelt, stretching out to dabble her fingers into the water. "Is this right?"

He nodded. "Are you ready?"

"I suppose so," she replied. "Do I need to do anything?"

"Concentrate on openness. Concentrate on letting the power of sun and moon flow through you. You are a conduit of magic. Do not fight it."

"I understand," she said, though really, she didn't.

The sky visibly lightened. The edge of a boiling red sun appeared at the edge of the wall. The moon still stood, high and bright above them.

"Me within you," Leontios intoned. "You within me. By the power of moon and sun, all things— through us—can be done."

Violet breathed the words, hoping they would have magical properties of trust she couldn't quite feel.

Leontios extended one hand and laid his palm on the crystal.

His hand grew warm in hers. Warmer. Hot.

Burning. His palm burned like fire. His fingers felt like branding irons. The heat spread up her arm into her chest and head. She was on fire.

Violet screamed in agony as the raw power of the sun poured into her body. She could feel herself turning to ash, flying apart. *Soon I will be no more.*

She had a vague sense of movement, though she paid it no mind, completely subsumed within the agony of her fiery death. That is until it ripped Leontios's hand from hers.

She tipped backwards onto the mossy ground and sprawled, panting. By pure instinct, she laid her burning hand onto the cool, moist earth and sighed as it soothed her.

When Violet opened her eyes and looked up at the moon, she noticed it had faded to a pale white silhouette as the sun became fully visible on the horizon.

Rise, woman. The words exploded in her mind. *Rise and stand. You have a mission to complete. Without your priest, you will die alone in the desert, and all you have risked for will come to naught. Rise and fight.*

"Fight?" she whispered. "Fight what?" She sat up slowly, willing her eyes to focus. Hearing awoke first. Thuds and grunts. Snarled words in a language she couldn't quite understand. Then, her eyes returned to life.

Before her, a familiar figure had tackled Leontios onto the ground. Something silver flashed.

A knife. Oh, God. He's trying to kill Leo. She sucked in a deep breath. Though her body ached and throbbed, she rose to her knees, wobbling and shaking.

"Azaan," Leontios barked, "what are you doing? You must stop."

"No," their driver shouted. "No, I cannot let you."

"We must diffuse the crystal. It's going to rupture."

"Good!" The man reared up, knife poised to plunge into Leontios's chest.

Violet didn't wait to see what would happen to a man whose essence was leather and paper if a knife plunged in. She crawled quickly to her dropped satchel and dug inside. The contents dug painfully into the burn on her palm, but she ignored it, drawing out her derringer. Bracing it on her aching skin, she aimed at the interloper who had… *Saved our lives, I suppose,* she thought.

Leontios also moved quickly. When Azaan leaned up, he interposed a bare foot and drove the man back.

Perfectly silhouetted against a burning red backdrop of sunrise, he provided a target Violet couldn't miss.

She fired the derringer.

Her injured hand trembled so that, instead of

slamming into Azaan's chest, the bullet dug into his upper arm near the shoulder joint.

Blood sprayed, flying in Violet's direction, splattering on her skin. It scorched, but after the burning she'd just experienced, the heat of lifeblood barely registered as warm.

Azaan roared and clutched his arm. The knife fell from his hand and stuck into the earth, nicking Leontios's leg as it went. Blood black as ink oozed into the mossy ground.

Azaan slowly sank forward on top of Leontios.

Seemingly unfazed by his injury, Leontios pushed the attacker off him and stood. "What are you doing?" he asked.

"Arrrrgggggh," Azaan growled. He lunged after the knife with his wounded hand, but Leontios kicked it away.

"You stop," Violet shouted, aiming the pistol at Azaan. "I have one more bullet ready for you."

He laughed bitterly. "As if that would help." But still, he subsided onto the moss, his face drawn in lines of pain, anger and resignation.

"What are you doing?" Leontios asked. "Why are you trying to stop us?"

Violet quickly put together the bigger picture of what she had observed. "He wants us to fail. He wants the crystal to rupture. He's been following us since we rode in his car. Isn't that right, Azaan? Even earlier. You tried to lose us at the market. You tried to divert us with promises of camels and guides. Anything to keep us from coming here. Why?"

He scowled at her but didn't answer.

"It was you all along, am I correct?" Leontios asked. "It was you on the train. You followed us to Cairo, and you have been stalking us through the desert to Skeon. It was always you."

"That would make sense," Violet commented. "The other man on the train, the freedom fighter, called him Ajnabi. Foreigner. Even though you've sided with them, you've always had another motive, haven't you?"

The man turned to look at her through dark, haunted eyes. "Yes."

"How do you know what we're doing, and why are you trying to stop us?" Leontios demanded

Azaan scoffed, clutching his arm as fresh spurts of blood burst forth. Already, an alarming pool had gathered beneath him. "I could *smell* you, *Master.* How could I forget your face? No passage of years could compel me to forget. No change of bodies. Your face is the last thing I saw before I died and did not die… the first time. As if I didn't know Leontios's energy from the first moment," he sneered. "What else could I do but follow you and seek my long-delayed revenge?"

"Eithon?" Leontios breathed.

"So, you figured it out, did you? About time."

"But how are you still here? I... I killed you when I destroyed Skeon."

"Oh, no, you didn't," Azaan—Eithon apparently —laughed bitterly. "I wish you had. You separated my spirit from my body and left me adrift. Alive, conscious and without a body to inhabit. I became a ghost. And as a ghost, I have wandered, alone, through the last four thousand years. Unable to touch another person until I learned to steal bodies. You were once a decent man, Master. If you have any decency left in you, do not do this. Let the crystal go and take me with it. It won't be long now."

Violet could imagine it—to be trapped, bodiless and adrift for centuries, unable to connect to another person—and the thought hurt. Compassion welled up. "That's dreadful." Setting her gun carefully out of his reach, she approached.

"Be cautious, VioletWarren," Leontios warned. "This man is dangerous."

"Yes," she replied, "dangerous like an abused animal. Like a beloved pet thrown out to fend for itself without skills or resources. He's feral, and that's sad."

"He has violated many others," Leontios warned her as he hauled himself to his feet. "What happens to the person when you steal their body, Eithon? Are you killing them?"

"Not precisely," Eithon rasped. Though he

sounded physically strained, his delivery remained calm. "Their personality remains alive, and we share a certain intimacy. It is true that they did not ask for it, and it takes much time for them to accept my leadership. In that sense, my presence is a sort of violation or perhaps invasion. I do not murder them, but I do make them my slave."

The spray of blood from his shoulder slowed to a sad trickle.

"That's a bad injury." Violet dragged a small bottle of alcohol out of her satchel and approached. "I need to clean it."

"Don't bother," he replied. Clearing his throat, he spat, and blood-tinged sputum trickled onto the ground. "It is a fatal wound. Cleaning it will not matter as I have already lost more blood than this body can sustain, and it will soon overwhelm me."

"You're so calm," she commented.

He nodded. "I have died so many times, in so many ways, that this is not the worst. It does not even hurt. The shock is blunting the pain." With each word, his voice grew thinner.

"And the man you have stolen? Is he afraid?"

"He is." Eithon's face grew ashy. "He, of course, has never died before. I am helping him to understand that this is not so bad."

"But he is young, and this is not what he expected." Leontios scowled.

"I also did not expect to die young, let alone become a bodiless shade. No one gets to choose."

"And what will you do once this body is dead?" Leontios demanded. "Will you go and steal another."

He laughed bitterly. "I will take Violet," he replied. "You will not be able to destroy the crystal without her. Though as badly as you were doing before, it seems like you would not be able to either way. Once the crystal bursts, I'll be free."

"You do not know that this will work either," Leontios pointed out. "As you say, you have died many times. Why would the crystal make a difference? More likely, you would be once again bereft, but with everyone nearby dead, it would be much harder for you to find a body to steal."

Eithon coughed. A dribble of blood ran from the corner of his mouth. "Damn. What then shall I do? I cannot go on this way. It is torture. How will you fix it, Master, since it is your fault? You owe me peace."

Leontios swallowed audibly. His face shuttered, and his tattoos crumpled into wrinkles of distress. "I know something to try. When I released my spirit into an object—my book—I was insensible. I had no awareness until Violet awakened me. I can embed your ghost into an object, in the crystal itself. There, you will remain forever. It is not true death, but it will feel the same. You can be at peace forever."

"Why should I trust you now?" Eithon demanded, his voice rough and thin.

"Allow me to try, my friend," Leontios urged, his face twisted with guilt and horror. "I did not mean to harm you, and you are right that I am responsible. Please, do not harm my Violet, nor all the innocent people near and far. I am still in my full power. I will help you be at peace. Will you but let me try, Eithon? You trusted me once."

Eithon released a rasping breath. His fluttering eyelids stilled, eyes staring. A rattling breath eased from his lips and he went limp.

Violet rose quickly and backed away from the corpse. "Uh, Leo, can you move his ghost into the crystal now? I don't trust him."

"Of course." He regarded his arm with intense scrutiny.

Something white and wispy floated in her direction. "Leo?"

"One moment, please, Violet," he mumbled before uttering several words she did not understand. The wisp zoomed away from her and disappeared into the rugged surface of the quartz chunk.

She sagged, sitting back down hard on the moss. "What the *hell* just happened. Who was that?"

"My former apprentice," Leontios explained. "He explained more or less what happened, though I wonder if you were able to make sense of it."

"Not in the slightest," Violet replied. "You killed him?"

Leontios nodded. "He begged me to. Egyptians were not kind to their enemies. He wanted a swift and merciful death. I tried to give it to him. Apparently, I failed." He lowered his eyes.

Violet crimped her lips. "I imagine, given the stress of the moment, you weren't at your best."

"I was not," Leontios agreed. "Eithon was my friend. My student. My successor. Also my nephew. I subjected him to a fate worse than death." He swallowed hard, his voice rough. He walked toward her, not with any obvious intention. Plunking down on the moss beside her, he reached out.

She enfolded him without thought, drawing his head down onto her chest and stroking the silky blackness of his hair. He shook in her arms. "I'm sorry, love," she murmured. "I can't imagine how that must hurt. Shhhh. Shhhh. Let it go. You don't have to be strong all the time."

He sobbed. Tears soaked into her shirt as she cuddled him close, stroking his hair, his back. "It is too much," he choked.

"I know," she said softly. "I know. You've endured more than anyone was ever intended to. I don't know how you've held on this long." Long minutes passed as the day grew brighter and the sun beat down.

A bead of sweat formed on Violet's forehead.

The sun's fiery red eye, still low on the horizon but growing hotter by the moment, seemed to dig into her. "Leo, can you move? It's too late in the day to be out in the sun. We need to get to shelter." She urged him upright.

"We must remove the body," he said raggedly, his voice breaking on every word. "If we leave him here, he'll be stinking by sunset."

"Oh, dear." Violet sighed. "Must we bury him? That's a lot of work in the hot sun."

Leontios shook his head. "No need," he rasped. Clearing his throat, he forced out, "just lay him outside the city walls. The vultures and the hyenas will have him picked clean in no time. It was what we always did. Honored the spirits of nature by nourishing them with our bodies."

"That's… very different," Violet said.

Leontios sighed, and when he spoke, he sounded steadier, as though having a concrete task had anchored him. "If he had remained and died in his original body, even his bones would be long gone. This is the nature of life, Violet. All die, and in their dying, they provide life to many. It is our destiny and not a fate to be avoided. Outliving your lifespan is no blessing."

She frowned. "You have as well."

He nodded. "But I have no awareness of it. From the day I died until now, I remain a man in my prime, and no time at all seems to have passed.

I can only imagine how terrible it must be to live on and on…" he shook his head. "Never mind about that. I cannot think about it all at once. Let us move his body out of the city and then settle down for a few hours. We must come up with a new plan."

Violet gulped. "Let me drink some water first. Is the water in this pool good to drink?"

"Probably better than good," he informed her. "Though not as infused with magic as it once was, a small trickle is still getting in. Raw sunlight and moonlight filter through this water, turning it into an elixir. Beyond that, as you can see, it comes from a natural spring deep in the earth. Unless something terrible has happened to it over the centuries, it will still be clear and sweet. Is your vessel empty?"

"Nearly," she replied, digging the canteen out of her satchel and draining the last lukewarm drops with a frown. "Let's get him out of here and then wash up. I've never touched a corpse before, and I'm far from comfortable doing so now."

"Then let us dispense with the discomfort quickly." He extended a hand to her, and she took it, levering herself to her feet.

The sun beat down on her, already uncomfortably hot. "Shall I take the head or feet?" she asked as she dipped her canteen into the cool water. Capping it, she hung the bottle across her torso.

"The feet," Leontios said. "The head is heavier."

Though she wondered if even the relatively lighter feet might not be too much for her, Violet obediently approached the corpse. *I killed this man,* she realized, and the thought set her stomach churning. *I shot him, and he bled out and died. I've never killed anything larger than a mosquito or a fly, yet I ended the life of a fellow human. A person I once spoke to and did business with, and I didn't even have a second thought. How was I able to do it?*

She stooped on legs that felt steadier than she would have expected and grasped his boots. It seemed her years hefting large chunks of pottery and stone had strengthened her more than she had expected, for even though the man's lower half did feel heavy, she had no trouble hoisting him, so his bottom lifted away from the ground.

"Oof," she commented. "Dead weight isn't just a saying, is it?"

"It is not," Leontios agreed, grunting as he tucked his arms under Eithon's and hauled him into the air. "It is fortunate Eithon selected a host who was similar in build to the way he used to be. A heftier man would not have been pleasant to carry in this heat."

The upward movement revealed the face to Violet, and she shuddered at the wide-open mouth and lolling, filmy eyes. *We must have sat longer than I realized.* "Let's call this poor fellow a victim, can we?"

she suggested. "Host implies an invitation that was never extended."

"Agreed. I hate to think that someone I once entrusted with the future of my people went so far wrong, but I suppose, under such duress, it is difficult to judge."

"I agree. I don't like it, but I can't even begin to imagine what I would do after centuries of not even being able to touch another human. Or object. Or anything. I hope he finds this sort of death enjoyable."

"I hope," Leontios disagreed as they approached the mouth of the tunnel, "that he finds nothing at all."

"That's what I meant," she agreed. "I find nothingness hard to grasp. That's all."

"It is," he replied. "I have experienced it, and I cannot understand or describe it because it is... nothing. There is nothing to describe except..." he trailed off.

"Except what, Leo?" They ducked into the tunnel, and thick blackness engulfed them. Though the sun outside grew brighter and brighter, inside this rocky structure, it quickly lost power. Fumbling in the growing darkness, Violet had to trust Leontios's muscle memory—while he walked backwards—to keep them from bumping into walls.

"Except I feel like," he said, calm as though they were sitting at a picnic, "at times I had almost an awareness. A soft touch. A warm embrace. A sweet aroma. Like a dream of a dream."

"Perhaps you remember me reading you?" she released a giggle that had more than a hint of hysteria in it. "You know, when you were a book?"

"Perhaps," he agreed. "It is too hazy to tell, but I should have been utterly insensible, and yet, I felt. Not through all that time. I mostly have no awareness at all of the years and centuries passing. But I do feel like I slept a long time, and during that time, someone talked to and touched me. It could be that I began making my way towards consciousness when you found me."

Violet bit her lip, not sure what to do with that information. "Um, I need a break. Can we set… him down for a moment?"

She felt him move before she heard his answer and lowered her end of the burden in tandem. Rising, Violet rolled her shoulders.

"Are you well, VioletWarren? I know that a dead man is a heavy load."

"I can carry him," she replied. "I don't enjoy it, and it's becoming a strain, but I will be able to get him through the tunnel."

"And after?"

"After, I hope you know a cool, comfortable place to sleep. I can already tell today is going to be miserably hot. I would have thought March would be cooler. I saw mention of the Khamsin winds, but

I completely underestimated how hot it would be. Regardless, it's been a long night, and full daylight is no time to be out in the sun. Not anywhere in Egypt."

She heard him shift.

"Or the great city of Skeon."

"You are correct," he agreed. "I think I can arrange you a comfortable bed, so we had better continue so we can get to it sooner."

With a sigh, Violet crouched and hefted the dead man's legs into the air. They felt a hundred times heavier, and she grunted. "Move quickly," she urged.

Leontios scuffled backwards.

She could feel her strength ebbing moment by moment. A sleepless night. Minimal food. Stress, strain and confusion. Killing a man. *Oh, God. I killed him. He's dead because of me. Dead.* She sniffled. *Dragging this heavy corpse out through a pitch-black tunnel so jackals can scatter his bones.* Her breath caught.

"Are you well?" Leontios, damn him, didn't even sound winded.

"I'm running low. How long is this damned tunnel?"

"Not long," he replied. "I can feel the light around the edges of my vision. Can you not feel it, Violet?"

Now that he mentioned it, she could feel it, but she wasted no energy on words. Her arms began to shake, and each step grew slower and more painful. The atmosphere lightened. Brightened. Grew painful. Grew blinding. Violet's trembling limbs began throbbing. Her feet dragged. She stumbled into the light. Falling to her knees, unable to take another step, she dropped Eithon's stolen body unceremoniously into the sand.

"It was much to ask, Violet." Leontios knelt beside her, resting one hand on her back. Despite the blistering heat, his warm touch tingled through her. *Just imagine,* she thought. *If you weren't so prissy, you could wallow in his touch. Feel it on every part of your body...* For a moment, it sounded... wonderful. Miraculous. *And while you're giving away the last vestige of your future hopes, he'll be performing a magical ritual.*

Her ardor died. She closed her eyes against a sudden burn.

"We need to get back inside. Can you stand?"

Violet tried. She struggled upright... and fell. "I guess I gave away too much," she rasped.

The hand on her back slid around her waist, lifting her. Leontios's chest compressed Violet's back. She dropped her head onto his shoulder.

"Violet, I can help you, but I too have used much strength. I cannot carry you. Please, try to walk."

Violet drew in a lungful of dusty air. The aroma of minerals and pure heat sank into her. Leaving her upper body limp, she forced strength into her legs. Every step burned, but she persevered. *If we can make it inside the tunnel, we can rest. Got to get out of the sun.*

Though her eyes remained shut, she could feel the change in light quality around her as they reentered the tunnel.

A brief sensation of falling ended with her gently laid on a soft pile of sand.

Leontios collapsed beside her. He drew her fully against him, enfolding her with an arm around her waist and a leg over her hip. He said nothing, merely exhaled hot breath on her neck. The hairs rose, though the rest of her body remained limp.

In the distance, a jackal yelped. Another responded.

Violet gagged, scrambled to open her water bottle and drank, capping it again quickly.

"Are you well?" Leontios asked gently.

Violet exhaled but did not answer. She had no words left. No thoughts. Nothing that she could dredge up, not even to provide comfort to this dear man. Slowly, she drew air back into her lungs and just as slowly let it out. It trembled. Stumbled. Turned to a sob.

Leontios moved, straddling her for a moment before crossing to recline by her side. He leaned forward and touched his lips to her forehead.

The tender gesture destroyed her. A shudder

shook its way up from her diaphragm until her every muscle trembled. She pressed her face against the bare skin of his chest and released the day… the week… the year… all the years since her mother's passing in a flood of tears. Shattered dreams tormented her. Lost hopes. Faded wishes. The death of innocence and the passage of years. Coherent thought shattered and shattered again until only tiny fragments of Violet's once-meaningful life remained, useless as glittering chips of mica in the sand.

Into the fragmented death of disappointment, she became aware of warmth. Arms embracing. Lips kissing. Tears falling into her hair, even as hers fell onto his chest. Though everything she thought she had known, had thought she had wanted was gone, this remained. Her book. The one constant that had brought her through so much turmoil had grown arms to hold her. Lips to kiss her. Had become a man who desired her. *Maybe I was right before. Maybe I did sustain a head injury, and this is my dream while dying. I always wanted an adventure. Perhaps my mind has conjured one.*

Foolish nonsense teased through her mind, but she never stopped weeping.

Tears eventually faded to exhaustion and exhaustion to sleep.

CHAPTER 12

*V*iolet woke to the wonderful comfort of Leontios's firm, mostly bare body curled around her. His skin under her fingers felt cool and soft, though the wiry muscles beneath teased her with images of strength.

A slightly embossed sensation yielded its meaning to her curious exploration. A symbol of his ancient language. Though she did not know the words, she felt an irresistible compulsion to read his tattoos like braille. She ran her fingertips across his skin, exploring each shape. *If I could read these, maybe I could understand him better. Know him better. I would love it if I could. And—joy—he seems to want the same. If we can achieve this goal and not burn ourselves up or explode, maybe we can.*

Leontios stirred, perhaps aroused by her

questing fingers. His own hands began to move, reaching low to cup her bottom. She snuggled closer, her hands sliding away from his chest to his shoulders, and she leaned in close.

He needed no prompting. Without hesitation, he laid his lips on hers. A kind of warmth born more in the heart than in her perspiring body rippled through her. Her body, already relaxed from sleep, seemed to melt as though she could dissolve completely with him and be remade as something new. Her knee bent of its own accord, coming to rest on his hip.

He hitched her forward more, so she could feel the fullness of his sex against her mound. Her intimate folds moistened. She opened her lips, teasing his with a swipe of her tongue. He yielded easily so they could slide together.

A sensation of languid heaviness spawned low in her belly and spread downward.

Leontios jerked his hips forward involuntarily. A groan escaped his throat. One hand left her bottom to slide up her torso and cup her breast. The touch elicited a riot of tingles from the arches of her feet to the roots of her hair. Her nipple tightened, and he thumbed it gently.

"Aaaaah," she sighed, caught between the urge to act and the need to surrender.

"Do you want me, Violet? Please, tell me you do. Tell me you no longer doubt me."

Violet froze, ardor shattered. "Why did you have to go and say that?" she groused. "How can I not doubt you? I've known you for a *week*. Less, really. That's not much basis for anything. Yes, I like you a lot. I'm attracted to you, as our currently compromising position shows, but I can't *not* doubt someone I just met. That would be insane."

Leontios drew back. "I am not suggesting that we have laid a foundation for a lifelong love in a week, or that we have shared experiences on which to base that lifetime. I only ask if you have basic trust in me, that you know I do not wish you harm."

Violet looked into his face—or tried to. Deep shadows obscured his features, but it didn't matter. She knew what she would see. His shattered disappointment.

I've seen it so often already, and yet he keeps coming back. Is it only because I'm the sole familiar face in this century? Or is there something more? He acts as enamored as I feel. But is it true, or does he just want me for his ritual?

"I trust you wish me no harm, Leontios, but that doesn't change anything. Remember, I didn't grow up in Skeon with its permissive attitudes toward sex." Only the near-total darkness permitted her to say the word so bluntly. "I was brought up that a respectable woman remained untouched until marriage. Many men have tried to claim my body, citing reasons ranging from my advanced age to wanting to be 'part of my family' which means closer to my father's wealth and connections. No one has ever desired me for myself."

She felt rather than saw him approach. Felt his compelling presence touch and then sink into her. He drew her fully against his body.

She tried to remain stiff in his embrace, but she couldn't. Her body felt what her mind rejected—that the safest place on earth was here in his arms.

"That is a sad commentary on this era, Violet. You deserve—like every man and woman of good heart—to be loved. You require no extra incentive nor any foolish persuasion."

Her heart melted, just as her body had done, but still, her mind resisted. "You want something from me too, don't forget. You want me to do some kind of arcane magic with you. Give you my body so we can perform a ritual. Maybe it's selfish of me to resist when so much is at stake, but don't I deserve more than this too? You don't want me for me either. You want me for the mission. That doesn't feel better."

This time, Leontios stiffened. His arms fell away. "I do not understand, perhaps because I am not from this place and time, but I would never force anyone. And I am not forcing you now. We come together because we cannot help it. Surely you must know this is true."

"I admit it," she agreed. "My desire to be close to you is… hard to describe or explain. I am not opposed to exploring it in time. But in time, Leo. Not under pressure. Not before it's even appropriate to mention a commitment, let alone make one."

"Then I will make another arrangement," he replied, resigned and sad. "Come. We should leave this tunnel. The palace is more comfortable, and I will need more rest. Besides, we should eat and drink. Is there any food left in your pack? Mine is growing depleted."

"I have food," Violet replied. "Two empty pitas and some figs, not much more."

"When night falls, we will have to explore the area around the pool. Once, many foods grew here; we even had a palm grove, as you can see. The wild descendants of these foods may remain."

"That sounds wise," Violet agreed. She knew her voice sounded painfully neutral, but she had to. Inside, she felt like she was bleeding." *And why not? I want nothing more than to be close to Leontios, and yet I can't stop myself from rejecting him, even knowing how much rejection he suffered during his lifetime. His Ellani must have been a very silly woman to have such a glorious man as her husband and hurt him over and over for the touch of another.*

"And what are you doing?" a sly voice inside her mind asked. "You are not even hurting him because you love someone else. You're hurting him because you fear your own desire. Fear losing yourself to someone you know would not hurt or even judge you. And you want him. You want him to overthrow all your defenses and force himself on you the way the men back home would have done. Only he won't because he's decent and he values your willingness. So why are you *really* not willing?"

Violet did not answer the arguing thought. She couldn't. She had no answer to give. Only a lifetime of training that fought with every breath against being indecent, even though it felt like the most natural thing in the world.

In silence, they traversed the tunnel, which seemed shorter this time, and stepped out into a blinding light that obscured the courtyard and its glittering pool.

Violet raised a hand to shade her eyes, but it was no use. The sun had traversed its path halfway across the heavens and stood nearly at its zenith, illuminating the white of the stones, the pale gold of the sand and the glittering luminescence of the water and the crystal. "Aargh," she protested.

"I know. Skeon in the full sun is too much to bear. Come. Walk with me." His hand clasped hers, and he led her away. She followed his lead blindly, eyes tight shut. His fingers laced through hers, and her heart skipped a beat. Her feet lost rhythm, and she stumbled. Even now, despite all she had done to hurt him, he still touched her as a lover, using the language of his people to show how much he cared. "Easy, Violet. Stay close to me. I will lead you."

Though she would have thought herself all cried out, another sob fought to escape her chest. She held it in, and it tore at her. Her pain. His pain resonating in her. Always alone. Always rejected. She gulped. His very thoughts resonated in her mind. In her heart. She stumbled again and nearly fell.

"This is not working," he said softly. "Come closer, VioletWarren. I will not let you fall." He tugged her forward against his body and embraced her, one arm around her waist.

He used my full name. He had just begun calling me Violet regularly, and now he's back to formality. Her exhalation sounded more like a wheeze. Her pain—his pain—sank deeper into her. A tear ran down her cheek. She lifted her hand to scrub it away, but another followed. Then another.

She became aware of a change in the pitch at which the crystal was humming. It had grown higher, fully into the audible range. Strident and shrill, it shrieked for attention. For relief. She could understand how it felt.

The quality of the light behind her eyelids changed, became less intense. Leontios urged her to a seat on a cool, soft surface.

Without thought, she fell backwards, intending to lie down. Strong hands caught her.

"Careful, Violet," he said. "There is a wall near your back. I do not want you to injure yourself."

But I injured you, she wailed inside herself. *I injured you, and you don't retaliate. You don't get angry. You just accept it and keep on being so kind I don't know what to do with myself.*

Of course, her words remained trapped.

"If you wish to lie down, go this direction." He urged her sideways until she lay stretched out on her side. "Now, I will retrieve our packs, and then we can spend the heat of the day at rest."

She heard his trousers swish as he walked away.

Violet rolled to her belly. Her canteen dug uncomfortably into her flank. She tucked her face into the crook of her elbow and released the tears.

In time, Leontios returned. She could feel him moving around her. Could hear the soft thuds of him setting objects on the floor.

He reclined near her and drew her against his chest again. The feeling of his soft skin under her fingers broke through her restraint, and she cuddled against him again.

"I do not understand," he murmured into her ear, "how you reach for me even though you are angry."

"I'm…" she sobbed. "I'm not angry." Sob. "Not at you." *I'm angry at myself. At my upbringing. At everything that gets in the way of this.*

Though she didn't say the words, he seemed to

understand. Cradling her against his chest, he stroked up and down her back with gentle fingers.

I love you. The words resounded in her head.

It couldn't be. Didn't make sense.

It doesn't matter. Some things are bigger than sense.

In time, Violet calmed. Again, being in contact with Leontios's skin felt right in ways she struggled to explain. She exhaled, releasing tension.

"You should drink some water," Leontios suggested. "You've spent more in tears today than we did in sweat across our entire journey through the desert."

She swallowed. "I suppose. I'm sorry."

"It is not surprising," he replied. "Much has happened in few days. It is no surprise that you are emotional. I have not been calm myself."

She smiled, though it felt quite watery and insincere.

"Now, Violet, since you are done for the moment, you must eat and drink, and then it is best to use our daylight hours to sleep. If you are not tired, I pray you let me rest. I have much to do and too few hours until the sun sets again."

At last, Violet opened her eyes. The cave's heavy overhang dimmed the blinding sun to a tolerable level. Deep shadows hung over them like twilight. Further back in the cave, blackness obliterated sight, but she could hear water splashing. The softness beneath her turned out to be moss as thick as carpet.

"This is the palace?" she asked, looking around at the gloomy interior as she unlaced and tugged off her boots and stockings. The cool moss felt marvelous under her hot feet.

"I told it you it was," he replied mildly.

"Yes, you did," she said. Rising, she retrieved her satchel and pulled out bread, which she bit into without excitement. It wanted to stick in her throat, and the drying crumbs made her aware of a burning thirst. Her bottle still hung around her chest, and she quickly unscrewed the lid and took a deep swig. Nearby, Leontios also seemed to struggle with a mouthful of desiccated food. Coughing, he gulped down water and sighed with relief.

"The water is amazing," Violet said. "It's so… fresh. I don't know how else to say it. I can taste that it's wholesome."

He nodded. "It is an elixir, as I said. It imbues life like no other water can. I am so glad it has retained its potency for all this time."

"It's a good thing the water is still potable. We were restricted to very dry foods in order to keep them safe."

"And that makes it all the more important to have abundant water."

This conversation is foolish and inane, she thought. *Can we think of nothing better to say?* "Um, Leo?"

He choked down another unpleasant mouthful and chased it with a swig of water. "Yes, Violet?"

"Um, what will you do? If I'm not able to work as your priestess, how will you drain the crystal? There's too much space between it and the pool. You can't reach it alone."

"Correct," he agreed. "Furthermore, it requires the power of moon *and* sun. I can only harness the sun."

Violet bit her lip. "And it's getting worse, isn't it? It sounds terrible."

"It is terrible. I doubt we will get another chance. If it lasts through one more day and night, I will be amazed."

Violet inhaled sharply, or she tried to. Her nose, clogged from crying, turned the gasp into an inelegant snort. "So, then, what's your plan? How can you fix it alone?"

"I cannot," he told her bluntly. "It requires two working as one: the moon and the sun; man and woman. Light and dark. I must have a high priestess. Thankfully, I have that opportunity in spite of your reluctance."

"How?" she demanded. "You can't walk back to Cairo overnight and start interviewing prospective priestesses."

He crooked one eyebrow at her. "Of course not. Remember, when the Egyptians invaded, Ellani was killed. Shot with an arrow before my eyes. I… I could not let her go. I preserved her spirit. She is there inside your satchel. I can bring her back. We can perform the ritual together. You need not worry. All will be well."

Violet took a sip of water as her feelings roiled. "So, you'll bring her back, tell her that over four thousand years have passed, make love to her, and at sunrise, perform your ritual?"

He nodded. "In essence, yes."

Violet said nothing.

"Does this not suit you? You must understand how important this is. What remaining choice do I have but to bring back my wife?"

The word wife slammed into her with the force of a bullet. It tore through her psyche. *If he brings her back, he won't need you anymore, and while their culture allows him to love one woman while married to another, yours doesn't. Nor would your heart. It would be the end of this lovely thing we're building.*

Leontios's face suddenly appeared before her. She jumped back, lost her balance and tumbled onto the moss. The water in her canteen gurgled out.

"Violet, are you well?" He grasped her arm and helped her sit back up. "I can see that you have something to say about this. Would you please share?"

She shook her head. "What can I say? You're right. This is the solution to the problem. She can do what I don't know how to do. She has none of these emotional impediments. But… she doesn't love you. You said that."

"It is true."

"Doesn't that bother you? It bothers me to think about it."

"I accepted it long ago. We do not have time to coddle our feelings, however much we might wish to. If the crystal is not drained immediately, we will all die. I must do what I must do. This is all that is left of my homeland. Hundreds of thousands or more of innocent people are depending on me. If you cannot help, I understand. However, giving up is not an option."

Violet frowned. "I know." She swallowed again. A strange ringing sounded in her ears. It had nothing to do with the crystal. "Can I… can I try once more? Maybe this time…"

He shook his head. "You do not know how to release the bonds of your body and your time. You do not know how to be one with another person. There is nothing magical about intercourse, Violet, but it allows a stronger sense of connection. Without that connection, we are both doomed."

"Yes. Connection." Violet sighed. "Therein lies the problem. We have this fragile, barely formed connection. It's too much for me to be comfortable thinking of you reviving your wife and bedding down with her, but it's not enough for me to commit to the same."

"Then you must choose," he told her solemnly. "It must be one or the other. We have no time for third options. If you cannot allow this intimacy because of the rules of your society, I accept that. But it means I must revive Ellani. If you care for me and do not wish to see me in the arms of another, so be it, but then the ritual falls to you. What do you choose?"

She shook her head. "It's so hard. They both seem like impossible options. I suppose… no… I don't know. Is it so much to wish the first time I share such an intimacy, it would be with someone who loves me?" She sniffled but fought down the sobs. She'd cried too much already.

Leontios knelt before her, laying his palm on hers. She laced her fingers through his without a second thought. "Is that why you are upset, Violet? Because you think I do not love you? You are wrong. So wrong."

"Leo, come on. You're, well… you're wonderful, but we barely know each other. How can you say that?"

He chuckled, his eyes crinkling in the corners. "After what I have experienced, time has little meaning. Besides. Do you remember our first meeting?"

Curious where he might be headed with this line of questioning, she responded, "We've known each other a handful of days. I think it's safe to say I remember just about everything."

"The first moment, when I took your hand to learn your language?"

"Yes?" She responded to his question with a question of his own.

"I saw everything. Who you are to the fullest depths. Your soul. Your spirit. Your history. I admit I do not understand all that I saw, but I learned you, Violet. I learned something that amazed me."

"What is that?" she asked. The shine in his dark eyes set her heart pounding.

"You are the one. It makes no sense. Across the centuries. Across such distances. We should never have met. You should never have known I existed, and yet, you are the woman I waited my entire mortal life to meet. We were made for each other. I love you, Violet. You are more than my friend. More than my savior. We could truly be one if you would but allow it."

Violet's breath caught. She bit her lip, staring into his beautiful, black eyes. Eyes that burned with desire… for her.

He knows nothing of money. Steel wasn't close to being invented in his time. It wouldn't surprise me if Skeon predated the Bronze Age. The foolish impediments that bind men of my time mean nothing here. My fa-

ther's wealth and connections mean nothing to him. None of the shallow considerations of my era matter to him. He wants nothing from me but… me. He's looking at me like that because… because he wants me. Oh, God. It is love. What else could it be?

If she concentrated, she could feel, as before, how his soul seemed to slip past the bonds of his physical form and caress her. It ran along her skin. A touch that held all the love she'd coveted her whole life. A love meant only for her.

Pushed past resistance, she dropped Leontios's hand and launched herself at him. Throwing her arms around his neck, she hugged him.

He embraced her. "So, I should not wake Ellani then?"

"Please don't tease me," Violet begged. "I feel like my world has turned upside down… again. I'm getting dizzy."

"I am not teasing. I need to know how you would like to proceed."

She buried her face in the curve of her neck. "Don't wake her," she mumbled. "Don't. I… I'll do what I need to do for you. For us."

"Is it what you want, though?" he asked. "It is still, as you say, for a purpose."

That argument sounds hollower every time I voice it. "Does it really matter?" she demanded. "I want you with me. For that, I would sacrifice a lot. No man has ever moved me the way you do. So, tell me what you need me to do, and I will do it. For the future I need us to have."

"Sacrifice? Oh, this modern world," Leontios lamented. "Do you think I would sacrifice one moment of your pleasure? There is no need to choose. You will lose nothing."

"Except my virginity," she muttered, though the way her body again tried to melt into Leontios told her that this conclusion would have been inevitable. No matter the circumstances, this relationship would have progressed to either a hasty trip to the altar or this. Consummating their love long before any pastor or priest would accommodate them.

"What a strange thought. How can being as close to the one you love as two people can be function as any kind of loss?"

"Never mind me," she told him. "I think too much."

"No. I like that you are a thoughtful woman. This is not thought. It is fear. I cannot imagine why your people, your culture, have decided women need to fear love. I think there must be a nefarious purpose to it. But leave that aside. Lie down and let us come together. Not for any ritual. Not because the world depends on us, but because I am your man, and you are my woman, and we desire each other."

No longer willing to hurt them both, unable to

resist her own desire, Violet nodded and let Leontios ease her down onto the soft, soft moss.

The strident whine of the crystal invaded Violet's awareness, reminding her of why they were rushing. She tensed.

"No, no," Leontios scolded. "Relax, love. What do you fear? You know I will not abandon you nor disrespect you. This is natural and for us—I think —inevitable."

"I know." She sighed. "I'm also nervous about the pain."

He chuckled. "There will be no pain, love. What, have the liars who locked up one of the gods' greatest gifts to mankind in a veil of shame also told you that you will hurt?" He dropped to the moss beside her. "I have touched your body before. Did it hurt?"

She shook her head. "Of course not. But… um, that's not what's supposed to hurt."

Leontios's arms crept around her, and he began to work the buttons that held shut her loose, casual blouse. "Tell me this terrible myth, love. If you have never been touched, and yet you are this afraid, the story must be powerful."

His words confused her. "It's not a myth, Leo. It's common knowledge. Women have a… um a sort of thin membrane inside them called a hymen. Her first time sharing intimacy with a man, he breaks it, which causes pain and bleeding and proves that she was a virgin."

The last button surrendered to his clever fingers, leaving her covered only by a thin undershirt. Leontios cupped her breasts in his hands. "I know of this membrane, yes. It is very stretchy and, for most women, is easily circumvented with neither pain nor blood. Only a clumsy, skill-less lover would do such harm. Has it become common for men to selfishly take pleasure from women without pleasing them in return?"

Violet gulped and then sighed as Leontios began thumbing her nipples. Warmth streaked to her womanhood, wetting and swelling the tissues. "I think that's likely," she admitted. "At least the men I have known, men who want to own me, think that this…" she moaned, unable to contain the sound as he gently gripped one tender peak in each hand, rolling the sensitive nubs. "That this is something they can take from me. Like my inheritance. Like my father. Ohhhhhhh."

Leontios bit her where her shoulder met her neck. *No, it wasn't a bite. Did he… scrape his teeth over my skin?* He repeated the scratchy caress, and Violet's head fell to the side, allowing him greater access. The wanton pleasure of his touches was draining away her fear drop by drop. Slowly, she began to relax.

"Such a terrible, terrible waste," he murmured

against his skin. "To have a lovely, intelligent, wise and interesting woman like you and only care for superficial things."

"I suppose that's to your benefit," she commented. "It meant that, until I met you, I never felt more than the most passing attraction, and that was only to strangers I would never see again. No one has touched me."

"It would not matter to me if someone had. It would take nothing from this moment but your fear."

"This kind of thought is more than I can understand and surely not helpful in this moment," she told him.

"Ah. Well then, will it help if I were to tell you how lovely you are? How I desire you?" He eased the straps of her undershirt down her arms until the hot breath of air inside the cave touched her bare breasts.

"Oooooh. Yes. That would help more."

"And this?" Again, he cupped her, the fullness of her bosom overflowing his calloused hands.

"That helps most," she admitted, her voice a pleasured rasp. "Leo?"

"Yes, my love?"

"By the custom of your people... Oooooh." He plucked at her nipples, and the shot of sensation straight to her intimate flesh stopped her from speaking altogether.

He kissed the side of her neck and ran his tongue along her skin.

"By the custom of my people?"

"Could we… oooooh. Could we be considered 'mated' already?"

"Yes, easily. We only need to voice the commitment aloud. Would that make you feel more comfortable?"

"It would. I…" her throat closed up in surprise as one hand slid down her chest to the fastenings of her high-waisted trousers. "I think that would make me feel much better."

"Violet, it would be my pleasure to commit to you by the laws of *any* people. For me, it is a simple matter of saying that I love you and want to commit myself to you, which I do. If you feel the same, then we are committed, and no further ceremony is needed."

"I do feel committed to you," she admitted, "or I would not be here. I think… I think something bigger than us both intended this from the moment we met."

"Long before then, love," he told her solemnly as the buttons of her trousers surrendered to his manipulations. "I believe the gods meant us for each other from the moment I was born, if not from the foundations of the earth."

She exhaled in a combination of ardor and attraction. *It could be love. It will be. And far sooner than any rational person would believe possible.* And so, when the front of her trousers hung loose around her navel, she made herself lie still. Leontios eased his hand inside, on the top of her bloomers.

"Later, when all this is done, will you… will you marry me? You know, in my way?"

Leontios leaned forward and kissed her cheek. "I would be honored. Only tell me what you require, and I will do it for you."

She relaxed. How could she not when he was massaging her mound with the palm of his hand? It was the most intimate touch she had ever experienced. Her desire had increased so greatly that she could no longer think. Could only feel the connection. The power of his touch, of their bodies melting together.

"Leontios… Leo," she spoke in an urgent whine. "I need… I want…"

"Yes, love. Yes. I know. I know what you need, and I know how to give it to you. Will you remove these garments?"

Violet yanked the blouse off her arms and tossed it away. She wriggled her trousers down and shoved them off her feet. Her chemise troubled her more, as his manipulations had left it trapped and crushed around her torso. "Help me," she urged.

Leontios embraced her from behind again, grasping the offending fabric and tugging it upward. She lifted her arms and allowed him to remove it. Now, she only wore her bloomers, and from the new sensation of heat against her bottom, she realized Leontios had taken the opportunity to remove his trousers, and he lay bare and comfortable against her, eager to relieve the longing they couldn't prevent from growing between them.

"May I take this from you, Violet?" he asked tenderly, slipping his fingers into the waistband of her knickers.

Her breath whooshed out as she thought of the relief he could bring her. "Yes," she murmured. "Yes, please."

He eased the undergarment down her thighs, and she kicked it away. When he returned, he did not lie directly against her back but instead angled his upper body away from hers, both his legs between her thighs. He urged her to bend her knee up, revealing her intimate folds.

She gulped but obeyed, as eager to feel his touch as she was reluctant to admit her need for this great intimacy. *Perhaps it's just as well he can't see my face,* she thought.

She bit her lip as his hand landed gently on her bare bottom and eased forward. He cupped her mound once more, gently compressing the tissues. She groaned.

His fingers pressed at the seam of her vulva, and the tender folds parted easily, allowing him access to her slick interior. He found her opening and eased his middle finger past the entrance.

Violet whimpered.

"Yes, love. Feel me. Feel me within you. Your desire is great."

"Will you quench it?" she asked, her voice trembling and thin.

"No, never. I will stoke it like a fire. Love can never be quenched. It can only be strengthened and built up to ever greater heights." He eased his finger back and slid it deep again. This time, he angled toward the front of her body, exploring the interior of her passage. His thick erection bumped against her bottom.

Violet's breath caught. *If one finger feels like* that, *what about…*

She grasped his free hand, which had come to rest on her hip, and laced their fingers together, her palm against the back of his hand.

"Come this way," he instructed, drawing her hand around her flank and urging her fingers between her folds. "Show me how you best like to be touched."

Violet froze, feeling the blunt, sensitive point beneath her. "I… I don't know. I… it's not allowed. I mean…"

"By all the heavens, Leontios growled. "What have your people done to their women? Let no man touch you and do not touch yourself? This is mad-ness. Here, I will have to try. Tell me if something does not please you but be patient. This will not be easy if you cannot guide me."

He began to caress her, moving the aching peak in a gentle, circular motion.

Violet sucked in a breath. She could feel wetness surging, and a strange tension began to coil in her belly.

"That's good. Very good. Now, relax, love." His finger eased out of her, and she whined at the emptiness. Oh, but Leontios was not finished with her. This time, his slow penetration spread her wide.

Two, she realized. *He's got two fingers inside me. Oh, God.*

"Is this the membrane that had you so worried?" he asked hotly, pressing outward. "It is small and should prove no impediment to our love. Just relax, and I'll ease the way further."

Violet collapsed, her head pillowed on her arm, and allowed Leontios free reign to play with the intimate parts of her body. Every touch drove her pleasure higher. Her face burned. Her breasts tingled, and the tender flesh he was manipulating felt... like no words in any language she knew could ever describe.

In total surrender, she let him stretch and caress her, preparing her for the moment when they would merge their bodies. *You'll let him do that too, won't you? Without a single protest.* A small smile creased her lips as she realized she would, and she felt no more fear. Only eagerness to know her lover. To be one with him.

Long moments passed while Leontios expertly worked. And as he had promised, he stoked the flame of her ardor higher and higher until she feared she might catch fire in truth. A shudder ran through her from the roots of her hair to the soles of her feet.

He stopped.

"Leo!" she wailed, shifting her hips restlessly.

"I know, love. Trust me. I know you need relief. Soon. Soon. Feel me now." A blunt pressure entirely unlike the sweet touch of his fingers eased through her outer folds and began to penetrate her sex.

"Breathe slowly, Violet," he urged.

Violet sucked in air and released it in a noisy whoosh as Leontios braced his hand on her hip and pushed. Pushed again. Little nudges eased him past her hymen, and as he had predicted, she felt no pain, only an intense pressure that rode the line between pleasure and discomfort. "Keep breathing, Violet."

She released the breath she hadn't realized she was holding, and as the air exited her lungs, Leontios thrust once more, embedding himself inside her as deeply as their position would allow.

Violet groaned. She shifted her hips in hopes of

relieving the thick pressure, but there was no escape. And now, he reached around her again, stroking her clitoris in hopes of regaining her eager pleasure.

His fingers missed the mark a bit, compressing in a way that, while not uncomfortable, did not produce the maelstrom of sensation she'd experienced moments ago.

Violet bit her lip. She wanted more. Wanted the obliteration of thought and sense that she'd just enjoyed, but this wouldn't work.

Steeling herself against shyness, she grasped his hand and guided him.

"Hmmm," he hummed. "Thank you, my love. Is this better?"

She couldn't answer. The intense pleasure stopped her voice entirely. Her hips rocked back, wanting to push him away. Pull him deeper. Evade the intense touch or increase it.

She felt a pulling sensation as Leontios withdrew and then groaned as he pushed back in again. His inward drive dragged his sex along an exquisite bundle of nerves inside her. He caressed her as he thrust, gently gliding in, pulling back and gliding in again. Violet burned hotter. Hotter. Fire radiated from her core out to her extremities. To every pore and muscle. Though she had never experienced it before, she knew *le petit mort* would soon arrive, and she both feared and yearned for it.

But no fear would restrain the wild pleasure that erupted and radiated through her body. She clenched down hard on Leontios's sex, and a soft cry of ecstasy escaped her mouth. He increased the speed and intensity of his thrusts, pushing her to greater heights of release until her body went limp.

Leontios grasped her hip again, increasing his pleasure with a gentle yet insistent rhythm. Violet offered no protest. She concentrated on drawing air into her heaving lungs. With the end of her orgasm, rational thought returned. She pondered the sensation of her lover inside her body, innocence giving way to experience in the tenderest, most loving act she could have ever imagined.

And yet, something felt incomplete. "Leo," she said gently, "Leo, I need to change this."

"What?" He stopped, poised at mid-thrust, confused by her comment. "Are you sore? Did I hurt you?"

"No, you were right. It doesn't hurt. I just… I want to see your face. I want to hold you."

"Ah. I will have to withdraw to change positions, Violet."

"I know. Please?"

He eased back, and if she had felt unfinished losing his finger, the loss of his sex was worse.

"Roll onto your back, my love."

She obeyed, parting her thighs and bending her knees.

He knelt between her legs and grasped her hand, guiding it to his sex. Her moisture slicked the thickened organ.

Understanding his unspoken command, she grasped him and aligned him clumsily with her opening. He surged back in, finding no resistance.

The change in angle stimulated her in a new way, and her back arched as she moaned. Her legs curled around his, and she wrapped her arms around his neck, drawing him down. She claimed his lips as he claimed her body, and for a fleeting moment, the idea of oneness dawned on her.

Leontios's back muscles tightened. His calves clenched beneath her feet. A snarling bark of laughter burst from him as he reached his own peak.

He panted as he drifted downward, his entire weight coming to rest on her body, chest to chest, their hearts pounding in tandem.

"I love you, Violet," he said softly.

"Hmmm," she hummed.

"Did you enjoy it?" He eased his sex out of her, and this time, she felt no distress. Their first encounter was over, but she knew there would be more, each one better than the last.

"It was lovely. Thank you for being so good to me, Leo. So patient." A sudden shyness arose. "And you? Did you enjoy… this? I was… pretty ignorant."

"Violet, my love, it was delightful. Remember that I am a scholar. Ignorance is not a deficit but an opportunity. Together we will learn how best to please you. I am eager to begin my study."

She giggled. "I am as well." A yawn escaped.

"We have spent much of our daylight rest. I do not regret a moment in your arms, but now, love, we must sleep. We have much to do when the sun sets."

She nodded, but her eyes were already closing. Violet settled herself on her side, cuddled close to Leontios's relaxed, naked body.

Sleep soon claimed her.

CHAPTER 13

The moon hung over the ruins of Skeon. Its light, mellow and pale, bathed the white rocks in a glowing luminescence. Violet looked up to see it, a narrow crescent with deadly sharp points on each end. Along the lower curve, a naked woman perched, one leg tugged up to her chest, the other leg dangling.

By pure instinct, Violet prostrated herself flat onto the ground. "My lady."

The woman jumped down, her body splashing into the pool. "Quiet, you," she ordered.

The crystal ceased its incessant whining.

"That's better. You've done well, Violet Warren."

Violet scoffed into the moss. "I killed one man and gave my virginity to another. Yes, it's been a marvelous day."

The woman sighed. "Get up. We cannot talk with your face in the mud."

Violet rose to a kneeling position, though somehow, standing before this elevated being seemed too presumptuous. She did take a long look at Leontios's moon goddess. As expected, her bare skin glowed from within, though it was not moon-white as Violet would have thought, but rather a tawny color that resembled the natives of the area. Long, curly black hair hung nearly to her ankles. Her curves flowed generously like fertility brought to life.

"Marvolo?"

The goddess giggled.

"And you called yourself Layla—night. How fitting. In Arabic, though?"

"It was a clue, though perhaps a bit too subtle. Now listen, Violet. You did not do anything wrong. You did what you had to do. You saved the man you love. You and he committed to one another, as you were meant to. The external rules and trappings of your society mean nothing under these circumstances. Admit it. Now that you know how love is supposed to feel, a man of your people would never do."

"I admit it," Violet said. "I still feel strange, though."

The woman shrugged. "Growing pains. You'll live. For a very long time, if you could only relax and let yourself. Haven't you hurt him—and your-self—enough by trying to be so rational? From the moment this book…" she gestured to the ground by Violet's knees, "came into your life, this outcome became your destiny. All that remains is to embrace it."

There, the familiar book lay in a pile of grass. Violet scooped it up and realized she too had nothing on. *Well, I did fall asleep naked,* she recalled. A tingle between her legs reminded her of the naughty pleasures she'd experienced.

"Stop thinking that way," the moon goddess ordered. "There's nothing naughty or wrong or bad about it. He's your mate by the laws of his people and soon will your husband by the laws of yours."

"My lady," Violet protested, face flaming, "not to be presumptuous, but could you not read *all* my thoughts, please. I'm trying to feel good about what has happened, but I'm still a bit… shy."

"Fair enough," the goddess said. "I won't pry. However, I do want you to work hard at not esca-lating your feelings beyond shyness. Don't reject him or what you have shared. Not again. Think of it as your wedding night if you must but let that con-nection grow. Let it blossom. You must. You have so much to do."

"My lady, if you can quiet the crystal, why don't you just…"

"Because it is your job. Yours and his. You must

succeed. If you do, you will achieve so much more than this simple goal. You will begin to create something new and special. Do you want a beautiful future rebuilding Skeon with your beloved? Popping into Cairo to explore the museum. Visiting the pyramids. Participating in digs and reading hieroglyphics? And at the end of those days, curling up in that lovely cave with your lovely man?"

Violet nodded. "That sounds marvelous. More than I could have ever dreamed."

"Then you must stop fighting it. What will the demands of Pittsburgh high society do for you here?"

"Clearly, my interest in following them is waning."

"Give them up faster. Embrace the magic. Embrace the rituals. Embrace Leontios, and all will be well."

Violet bit her lip.

"And stop doing that. You'll chap yourself to pieces in the desert wind if you can't keep your lips out of your mouth."

Violet released her bite quickly.

"It's time for you to wake up."

"Wake up, Violet. Night has fallen."

Violet sat up with a start. "Goodness." Unlike in

her dream, awake, her nakedness made her feel powerfully timid. She covered her breasts with one arm, her mound with her free hand.

"Be at ease, my love," Leontios urged. "You are lovely, and you are loved."

She sighed and let her arms drop away from her body. Wearing nothing more than a blush on her cheeks, she rose to her feet. Her legs ached, as did her arms, her back and her forehead. Oddly, her sex felt wonderful, apart from the clear indications that something momentous had happened to it. *Amazing. He was right. Maidenhood is a myth.* The rest of her, however, hurt badly. "Leo, do you have any treatments for aches and pains? We did a lot of manual labor yesterday."

"Yes, Violet. I know a remedy if it still grows in the courtyard. We should venture forth. Even if that one herb is not present, we must try to find food—I have tired of dry bread and goatmeat—and drink as much as we can stand. We have let ourselves grow too dry and may become ill if we do not take in more water soon."

"I agree to all that," she said, reaching for her clothing.

Then, she noticed Leontios striding out into the moonlight naked.

And after all, why not? There's no one here. No one knows we're here. No one knows that here even exists. The moon goddess doesn't care. So be it.

She stretched her aching muscles and walked out after her beloved. *My husband,* she reminded herself. *Almost.* As the moon beamed down on her, she realized that, in the extremity of the previous day, she had neglected to wash Azaan's blood from her. She frowned. *How on earth did I get so lost in my passion for Leontios that I surrendered my virginity with a man's blood splatted all over me? Good God.* She swiped at the droplets, only to find that not only had they dried to a disgusting crust, the movement caused agony to flare in her strained arms. A squeak of distress emerged.

Leontios turned, his flaccid manhood swinging with the movement, which gave her a rare opportunity to observe the parts of a man she had never before seen outside a sketch or a sculpture. He approached, slung an arm around her, and drew her against his side. Up close, she could see the tangle of images, glyphs and symbols etched all over his skin. He was marked from head to toe by the knowledge of his many years of study—and it looked glorious. "Are you feeling timid today, love?" he asked, embracing her. "I still love you. I still want nothing more than to spend every day that remains in this existence with you. Whatever dire predictions you feared will not be realized. Not with me. Not between us."

Violet bit her lip, remembered the warning, and released it. "I guess I am. On the one hand, I'm ready to believe that everything including fated love and magical crystals is real. On the other, you touched parts of me that no one has ever touched before, not even me. So, yes. I feel a bit timid… or maybe sensitive."

"It was lovely," he reminded her. "It will be again. I predict that someday soon, you will crave my touch as badly as I crave yours."

"I know I will," Violet said. "I can already feel the longing."

He tucked a finger under her chin and, comfortable as though he was born to it, lowered his lips to hers in a tender kiss. "Do not fear it," he urged. "Whatever those other men made you feel is nothing to do with this. With us. We are one, and nothing can come between us. This is just one more way to feel the oneness."

She smiled.

"And for now, if you wish, you can tell yourself that we were selected for each other by deities beyond the rules of mortal man. Made for each other. Here, in this garden, no one can touch us, and we are free to love each other as they intended us to. If that makes me your husband, I will not fight being so named."

She smiled. "Thank you, Leo. Now, let's find something to eat, can we?"

"Yes. Of course. Though you look so lovely with

the moonlight on your skin, I would be delighted to make a meal of you right now."

Her belly fluttered, and her thighs clenched. And then her stomach growled. She giggled. "Later. When I'm not splattered with blood and caked with sweat… and starving," she added as her stomach rumbled. "Come on. What might I expect to find here?"

"I can guarantee you dates. Just look at those luscious palms. There might be onions buried in the ground. Grapes along the wall or climbing the trees. We once grew grains like barley, but only outside the walls, so I doubt we will find much here."

"Is there anything I should be wary of, like poison ivy?"

"I do not know what that means," he replied. "Do be aware of Samwa. It can make you itchy, but as it smells and tastes repugnant, I do not think it will tempt you."

"Likely not," she agreed. "Um, I can't climb a palm tree, so I will hunt for grapes if you don't mind."

"Perfect." He hurried to the nearest palm tree and peered up into its branches.

Violet knelt beside the pool and slashed the cold, wholesome water onto her skin, washing away the remnants of the previous day's torment. Then, she crossed to the outer wall. As she approached the crystal, its strident wail threatened to shatter her eardrums. She clamped her hands over her ears. "Be easy, friend," she said to it. "We'll try again soon to help you. Just hold on. Hold on a little longer."

Above, the moon shone down, not quite full but almost. Its light seemed to beam directly into the crystal, and Violet swore she could see the vibrations rather than just hear them. She rushed past it, examining the vines that had climbed the far side of the wall. Sure enough, fat purple grapes clung to the stones. Violet gathered several bunches of the juicy, ripe fruit and carried it to the mossy spot along the edge of the pool. She set them down and moved on in search of something else to eat. After days of bread, meat and chickpeas, fruit sounded delicious, and the water burbling out of the cave tempted her terribly. She paused to dip her hands in the water and splashed her face again before cupping a handful to drink. It tasted like life. Life, greenness and wonder. She drank more and could feel vivacity pouring into her.

"What did you find?" Leontios asked, setting a bough loaded with dates next to the grapes. "Hmmmm. Delicious. I cannot wait." He reclined on the mossy bank and popped a grape into his mouth.

Violet grabbed a date. "This is so lovely," she commented. "Just think of all the produce we could sell in the souk if we could just deal with that crystal."

"That would be one option," he agreed.

"Does it make you uncomfortable to walk around naked like that?" Violet asked, getting an even closer look at his long, bare form, from the blue marks etched on the top of his feet to the symbols on his temples.

"Not particularly," he replied. "Clothing was minimal in Skeon. What you have seen me in is rather... formal and overdressed for everyday life. I prefer a simple loincloth."

"You're not wearing a loincloth," she pointed out, unable to stop herself from eyeing his penis.

He grinned with one side of his mouth and drew her closer. "You may touch it," he said. "I know you are curious."

Leaving her to decide her own fate, he plucked another grape and fed it to her.

She bit into the juicy globe, discreetly spitting a seed onto the ground. "I think I'll wait on that for now."

"Pity," he complained, popping a date into his mouth.

"Well, don't you need to save your arousal for the... the ritual?" she asked.

"You make an excellent point, love," he replied.

Violet reached out for another bite of fruit and then groaned as the muscles in her back ached.

"Here, chew this." Leontios plucked a leaf from a low-lying plant near the water.

Violet asked no questions. Merely set the fragment between her teeth, frowning at the bitter taste. "Is it a painkiller?"

"Correct." Leontios took on the didactic tone of a teacher. "In a short time, you should find the edge taken off your discomfort. For true relief though, it would be better to rub the sore muscles with oil."

"That also sounds marvelous. However, I don't think we have enough oil to achieve it and perform our ritual later. We'll need to return to Cairo to buy some. You know, after we take care of today's business. Maybe we can visit the bathhouses. I hear they're quite popular with tourists and locals alike. Get a good scrubbing and massage." She shivered at the thought and realized that, in all the excitement, she had forgotten the burning in her hand. Examining it by moonlight, she could not see any external injury, though she could still feel the stiffness and sensitivity as though it lay beneath the skin.

"I hope now that we are better bonded to one another, we do not experience such pain again. Remember, Violet. I can channel the sun but not the moon. You can channel the moon but not the sun. Only when we operate as a single being can both abilities flow through us unharmed."

"You say things I don't understand," she told him, frowning.

"Perhaps it is not necessary to understand how

it works," he informed her. "I only have theories myself, after all. It is enough that it works if you do not fight against it. You can see what fighting causes."

"Yes," she agreed. "Burns and pain. It's like a sunburn, only I can't see it."

"It exactly is a sunburn," he told her. "A sunburn of the spirit if that makes any sense. Here. Take my hand, Violet. You may use the unburned one if you like."

Violet reached out and laced her fingers through Leontios's. It felt right and natural as always to touch him.

"Now, open your mind. Put aside the rules and laws and discoveries of this current age. Know that, while some may be more useful than others, none are beneficial at this moment. Try to save them for another time. Magic is real. You have seen it, and you know it. I am real. I was your book, and you loved me then. Now, I am your man, and I love you in return. We have a special connection. We are one already."

His soothing words sank into her. His touch calmed her. The soft moonlight bathed her senses in a silvery sheen. If it weren't for the strident note emanating from the crystal, she might have felt perfectly at peace. More peace than she had ever felt in her life. *It's like Eden,* she thought. *Our oasis in the desert. Our mission and our goal. Our purpose and our reward. Life at its most primal and perfect.*

Without thought, she leaned over and kissed Leontios on the lips. No words marred their communion. Hand to hand, mouth to mouth, they bathed in each other's presence, and again the understanding of one rose in Violet. She reached for the meaning, but it slipped away. She let it go, caught up in embracing her beloved. Of their naked bodies shifting, shifting until they aligned on the soft moss. *It's like a honeymoon,* she realized. *Or it will be once we take care of that...* The droning of the crystal, like a thousand angry mosquitos, drilled into her awareness. It did not shatter their connection, but it did interrupt the moment a bit.

That is until Leontios slid one arm under the dip of her waist and pulled her flush against him. He released her hand to cup her breast.

"Already?" she asked, pulling back and blinking at him. "Shouldn't we wait until dawn is closer?"

"It matters little," he told her, his eyes burning bright in the darkness. "Remember, Violet. Intercourse does not confer oneness. Our union exists regardless. It has been in us from the day you picked me up in whatever dusty corner you found me and carried me home. Coming together only reminds us in a physical way that we are one. And it feels good. Relaxes the mind. It is important to be physically and mentally relaxed before attempting to interact with the crystal."

"I see," she said, though true understanding still evaded her. She knew intellectually what he meant, but a feeling of perfect surrender remained outside her experience.

"And you are still confused," he commented, stroking a strand of golden-brown hair over her shoulder. "Which is probably why our previous attempt failed. From what you are telling me, you have guarded your independence fiercely and for many years. Denying suitors access to your body was more than just a cultural expectation, was it not? After all, you have denied many other rules of your time. This was personal."

"It was," she agreed. "I didn't want to be used."

"Understandable. But that is no longer the case. I am not using you."

"I know you're not," she told him gently, reaching up to trace the tattoo on his temple. "I mean, here I am with you, naked and deflowered. I wouldn't have let anyone else touch me the way you did... the way you will again, am I right?"

"Again, and again." He leaned in to kiss her lips once more. "And again, and again. You enchant me, Violet. You are magical even if you do not fully believe in it."

She smiled and tugged him close again. He

cupped her bottom, dragging her against him so she could feel his growing erection.

Violet blushed and giggled, wiggling away and plucking a grape to feed to him.

"Shy, sweet lady?" he asked, one eyebrow raised. "I'll have you making new sounds before you know it."

"Here. Eat some dates. Stick your teeth together, so you stop teasing me," Violet suggested, trying for blandness but failing.

Leontios laughed. "You are so lovely when your blush. It travels across your skin so beautifully. How could I not wish to tease a few more blushes?"

Violet wrinkled her nose. *He's laying it on a bit thick… but I like it. Why do I? This kind of nonsense would have had me running from the room with anyone else.*

"It's because you know he's sincere," the moon goddess whispered into Violet's mind. "Those other men were trying to manipulate you. Leontios tells you sweet things because he loves you and wants you to know it."

The intrusion embarrassed her. To distract herself from her intense feelings, she claimed another kiss from her man. This time, she swiped him with her tongue, liking that she could be the aggressor with no repercussions. Leontios responded eagerly as always, letting her direct their kiss. He stroked her shoulder, her back. He cupped her bottom.

"I cannot stop wanting you," he breathed. "Let us retrieve the oil. Already, I sense that dawn is not far off." He hoisted himself to his feet and walked away, his lovely, firm backside tempting her. Glyphs rippled with the movement of the muscles.

Violet could feel the coming dawn as well. The quality of the darkness had begun to shift below the wall that separated the inner court of Skeon from the Egyptian desert beyond.

A flutter of nerves tried to rise. Their first encounter had been born of an overwhelming need to consummate their mutual adoration, but this one had been planned and had a purpose. On a deep level, that still bothered Violet a little, but the scream of the crystal overrode her objections. *No delaying. We have not a moment to spare. At least I know now that this… ritual won't be painful or embarrassing. He will make it sweet for me.*

She couldn't help but smile.

Only a few moments later, Leontios emerged from the cave, the flask of oil dangling from his fingers. Violet's stomach clenched.

He gave her no time to work herself up. Dropping to his haunches, he stretched out on his side again, pulling her close to quell her nerves with a wild kiss.

As before, when Leontios applied his purpose to seducing Violet, she found it easy to relax and succumb. His hands on her body felt like fate. His lips on hers spawned a sensation of love eternal.

Then, he shifted to sit crossed-legged on the mossy bank of the pool and urged Violet up in front of him. "Anoint me," he urged, taking her hand and pouring oil into it.

She dipped her finger into the puddle and ran her hands into his hair, streaking it across his scalp. He closed his eyes. "That feels lovely," he told her. His shoulders relaxed. She took her time, caressing his scalp and feeling the myriad tiny muscles let go.

Her eyes met his, and the passion in the dark pools drew her like a vortex. She could feel reality swirling away. Swirling, and she let it go. She fell into his eyes. Into his heart, which shone with love for her.

Love for me. He loves me. And I love him. It's so simple that it obliterates complexities. Everything will fall into place because it must. Because we have. She kissed his forehead and traced a heart around the spot with her oily finger.

Leontios moved then, pouring oil into his own hands. He laid a thick line along the part of her hair, and she shivered with pleasure.

Violet crossed the heart she had drawn with a thin line that ran up to the roots of his hair and down the bridge of his nose to his lips. He kissed her finger. *How strange and how lovely that arousal is simmering though we have only touched each other's faces. This isn't going to be nearly as difficult as I feared.*

Leontios rubbed his hands together, coating them both with oil. Then he ran his thumbs from her eyebrows to her hairline. It felt wonderful, and her head tipped back, revealing her throat.

He bit her, scraping her skin with his teeth so shivers ran through her body.

"Is it right to be enjoying the ritual so much?"

"Oh, yes," he replied. "We're meant to."

Reassured, she relaxed into the mutual stroking of oil over tender points on the skin. Giving and receiving. Loving and caressing. Leontios cupped her breasts with oily hands, gently squeezing and massaging. His palms compressed her nipples. His thumbs slid together over her heart.

Violet returned the favor, circling each of his nipples with her fingertip. She gently pinched each one, enjoying his pleasured gasp.

Her fingers slid lower, X-ing out a small pictograph between his belly button and his groin. Unable to resist the temptation, she oiled her entire hand and began to caress his penis. He hardened quickly from half aroused to rock hard and ready. She smoothed oil over the shaft and down onto his testicles.

"Gently there, love. It is sensitive," he urged. "But touch me. It feels so good."

With care, she cupped and cradled the sac, examining its velvety wrinkled texture and the sparse hairs that dotted its surface. Her beloved released an agonized groan at her exploration. He had no tattoos here. Not between the top of his pubic hair and the joining of his thighs to his groin. Only this small, so-intimate patch remained the lovely caramel color of his skin.

Leontios massaged her belly with his thumbs, compressing internal organs she had never realized had erotic power. Her vagina clenched in response.

He ran his hands down her legs to massage her sore feet deeply. She moaned in a combination of pain and pleasure as the tight knots released.

In a hurry now, she dabbled oil onto each of his feet and shifted, drawing him down on top of her. "I need you," she told him simply and without shame. "I need you right now."

Leontios pulled back, so he knelt between her thighs. "Let me be sure. You are very new at this, Violet, and I do not wish your direst predictions to prove true."

"You would never hurt me." She thrust her hips helplessly. "I know you wouldn't."

"I will not because I am careful, love. Let me test your readiness. The anointing was arousing, but I suspect you will need more before you are truly ready." He laid both hands on her vulva, parting the folds so the night-cool air kissed her fevered flesh.

Well-oiled fingers delved into her, gently pressing outward to lubricate and widen her passage. Slippery thumbs worked her clitoris, ratcheting her pleasure from latent to wild. Then, he shocked her by crouching down and covering her with his mouth. His tongue ran up and down the tender nub as though licking at a delicious confection. His fingers delved to her depths and rubbed sweetly. Violet longed for bedding she could grip to fight the passionate onslaught but found only cool, slippery moss beneath her fingers. She gouged it from the rocks below and tossed her head as Leontios attacked her most intimate places with tender violence.

Tension coiled in her belly, taut as a bowstring, bowing her back into the mossy rock on which she lay. Tighter and tighter the bowstring drew until she let it loose with a wail of unrestrained pleasure. She clamped down hard on his fingers, and her hips thrust upward, instinctively seeking more. Seeking *him.*

"Leo," she cried. "Leo, please… Please, now."

"Yes, love," he agreed, easing his fingers out. "Now, you're ready." He crouched over her, grasping his sex and feeding the tip into her clenching passage. This time, because he had loved her so recently, he had no trouble entering her fully in a single stroke.

She wrapped her legs around his waist and her arms around his back, drawing him down.

So interesting, she thought, or started to. Until the oil on her feet slipped on his bottom. She let them fall, coming to rest on his calves. He lowered his chest to hers, and the warm oil over his heart came into contact with the warm oil over hers. She could imagine, could *feel* his spirit slipping his body and oozing through the contact point into her.

The exquisite thickness of his sex extended her orgasm, built it to ever greater heights until she feared she would die of it. He braced his weight on one arm, and with the other, laid his palm on hers, asking in the language of his people for her to love him. She closed her hand around his as he began to move, to thrust into her with tender passion. Their oily palms provided another means for his spirit to mingle with hers. She could feel it. Could feel the *you within me* as it began to happen.

She whimpered and squirmed as he drove deeper and deeper into her yielding flesh.

"Me within you," he rasped, and she could see on his face how he had to fight to force the words out. The movement of his lips drew her attention to the sheen of oil there.

"You within me," she added, her voice a thin whine. Surrendered fully to the experience, she could feel Leontios within her. Within her body, her heart, her spirit. He possessed her.

That's not right, she realized. *It's not oneness, which is what we need. It's only him possessing me, but it should be me within him as well.*

She laced one hand into the back of his hair and pulled him down, kissing his mouth with eager ardor. At last, her spirit slipped from her body, sliding through the oil on their lips and entering into him.

"Hmmmm," he met her with a pleased hum. "Yes, like that, love. You within me." Then he fell silent as she tongued his mouth.

Me within you, she thought. *I know you can hear me, moon goddess. You within me. By the power of moon and sun, all things—through us—can be done.* At last, she believed it. Believed in the oneness that flowed between them. She was him. He was her, and it was meant to be from the foundations of the earth.

"I love you," she whispered against his lips. "I love you, Leo."

He backed up enough to look down into her face, his dark eyes burning with the adoration she could now feel, not just know. She could feel her love flowing up to him. Could feel the love in his passionate thrusts into her body and in the tender way her passage caressed its welcome guest.

In perfect alignment, they began the chant together. "Me within you. You within me. By the power of moon and sun, all things—through us—can be done."

Violet's core clenched down as an unexpected second peak gripped her.

Leontios clutched her hand as she gripped him. He laughed a barking laugh of ecstasy. Their bodies froze at the culmination of their passion. Their love swelled to new proportions, proportions too great for their bodies to hold. It spilled from them into the lush foliage of Skeon's inner courtyard. Into the palace. Into the pool. Into the crystal itself, which absorbed the energy, and its annoying whine ratcheted up to an alarming rattle.

Violet slowly relaxed into the moss, her body softening, but the sense of deep connection remained. *It really is part of us,* she realized. *It's what I've been seeking for my whole life.*

The darkness changed. Brightened, and a ray of sunlight shot toward the sky.

Leontios eased himself out of Violet's body and stood, extending a hand to her. "Come, love. We have a task to do."

Relaxed, replete and finally confident, Violet wrapped her hand around his and let him help her to her feet. Her legs wobbled. Her body shook. Leontios slung his arm around her and urged her against her his side, walking her to the edge of the pool closest to the crystal and helping her to kneel. She dabbled her fingers into the water.

Leontios kept his hand in hers and reached out.

"Again, Violet. Say it with me and know in your soul that it is true. Me within you."

She mirrored his thoughts. "You within me. By the power of moon and sun, all things—through us —can be done."

He touched the crystal.

The sun-bright heat flared in his palm, but his spirit within her buffered her from its brightness, allowing the energy to swirl into her without harming her.

Her spirit, with its barely understood connection with the moon, reached through him, through his hand to touch and draw moon magic from the crystal. She wrapped its foreignness around his heart, his arms, his hands, so it wouldn't harm him.

The connections snapped into place with an audible click. Leontios inhaled deeply and released his breath. Violet followed suit. Energy trickled through him and bounced against her hand. She shifted her grip, lacing her fingers through his. The power surged again. This time, it breached the barrier of her modern understanding and flowed through her. Through the channel she had created through him. Through the one he had created through her and into the pool. A trickle grew to a stream, a stream to a river. A river to a flood. The channels swelled, near to bursting with millennia of backed-up energy.

The stretching hurt. Violet whimpered against the pain.

It grew.

Nausea churned in her stomach. She arched her neck forward to vomit, and raw energy poured from her mouth onto the ground before her. It leaked from her eyes like tears. It dribbled like milk from her breasts. It forced its way from every pore. And still, the flood increased until every opening in her body flowed with power, and she was burned away, nothing but a vessel for magic left untended too long.

Too overwhelmed to scream, Violet used her failing strength to plunge more of her hand into the pool. *I'm dying. I can't survive this, but no matter. If I must die, I will drain this damned crystal with my last breath. After my last breath, I will drain it with my corpse until my flesh rots away.*

Father, I'm sorry I never found you. I love you. I hope you're at peace.

Through pain beyond the imagination of humanity, she knelt, immobile and aware, suffering yet feeling no regret. *One night of Leo's love was worth it.*

Centuries that probably lasted a minute each burned by as Violet bled raw magic, and yet she did not die. Subtly, she became aware that the flow was less. Still more than her body could sustain, but not as violently so. Another eon of agony and she perceived another reduction. Then another. Minute by minute, the flow reduced from a flood to a river. From a river to a stream. From a stream to a trickle and at last, it stopped.

Violet dropped Leontios's hand and collapsed onto the moss. Unconsciousness mercifully wrapped her into its dark embrace.

CHAPTER 14

A sense of movement drew Violet up to consciousness. Movement and pain. She screeched as every joint, every muscle in her body shrieked. Even her bones and teeth seemed ready to splinter.

The sun blasted down on her, and she realized her skin had already begun to blister. *How long have I been unconscious?* she wondered, but her mouth refused to form any question. Any sound other than an endless scream.

The movement continued, jerking on her as someone—Leontios, she realized—half dragged, half carried her toward the royal cave of Skeon. Toward protection from the sun.

It was far—so far—and he was mostly spent, but he still struggled on.

She tried to help, tightening her muscles to take some of her weight, but she couldn't. As she engaged a single toe, her agony flared, cutting off her cries in a choked sob.

Another sound cut into her awareness. A growl. Leontios expressing his pain, even as he struggled to get them both out of danger. *He could leave me,* she thought. *Save himself. I'm not strong enough, and after all that… all that… neither is he.*

But of course, he would not leave her in the sun to die. Of course, he must save her, and so he continued their agony. Prolonged it. Increased it with every rock he tripped on. With every fumbling step, until at last, the blessed shade of the cave closed around them.

He laid her on the cool, cool moss beside the stream that flowed from the cave into the pool, and with a splash, toppled into the water.

Violet wanted to reach out. She tried, but her muscles again fought her mind's command. This time, she fought back. The moss soothed her skin. The pain-relieving herb she had chewed still worked to blunt the edges of her agony. The knowledge that the water right beside her had magical healing properties propelled her beyond pain into action. She slid one hand into the water, and as she had hoped, it assuaged her pain a little. At least to the point that she could feel her tissues relaxing into soreness rather than outright fire.

Encouraged, she slowly made her way onto her side so she could dip her wrist in. Her arm. Another lunge. She toppled into the water completely. It felt like heaven, soothing her agony to an almost tolerable ache. Though she knew she was far from well, at least she could breathe again, and only whimpers emerged.

She remained in the water until the burn in her body turned to ice, and she began to shiver.

"Come, Violet," Leontios rasped in a pained whisper. "We must get out of the water now."

She tried, failed, her trembling limbs not wanting to emerge from the only source of comfort she could imagine. But the cold began to ache in its own way, and at last, she heaved herself out, crying softly with pain. Leontios joined her, drawing her against his body and curling around her.

"Rest, love. We did it," he murmured against her skin.

"It hurts," Violet whimpered. "Am I burned all to bits?"

"You have a serious sunburn on your back," he admitted. "I have no idea how long we were unconscious in the full sun, and of course draining the crystal took a large toll. We will recover with rest, food and lots of water, but right now, we are both badly injured."

"How can I rest?" Violet demanded. "I'm in too much pain."

"Do not move," he urged. "Do not move a muscle. Let your body relax. I am here, here with you. I have you. Rest."

His voice—still hypnotic though raspy with pain—seemed to sink deep into her. She let loose the tension she had forgotten she was holding. Her shivering stilled, and as he had promised, her pain didn't flare unless she moved. And when she lay still and relaxed in his arms, she found she could sleep after all. So, she did.

The moon had risen high, though not nearly as full as it had been when Violet woke. She found herself alone inside the cave, lying on a comfortable bed of moss. She tried to sit up and groaned as the aches in her muscles reminded her that all was not well. Still, she felt better than she would have expected. Also hungry. Though her aching throat spasmed at the idea of swallowing, she knew she would need strength for healing, and so she rolled to her belly and rose to her knees, crawling from the cave in search of something to eat.

She found the bounty of fruit she and Leontios had gathered the previous night. *Was it, though? I have no idea how much time has gone by.*

Leontios himself lay beside the pool, stuffing grapes into his mouth, one after the other. She dragged herself over to him and claimed a handful of dates.

A strange sense of loss hung heavy over the garden, and she realized it was the loss of noise. The crystal lay silent. No, not exactly silent, but its barely detectable vibration caused no distress.

"I'm not looking forward to wrangling that thing again," she said before a fit of coughing cut off her rusty words.

"I think we can let it be for a few months," Leontios agreed while she scooped up water and drank it. "If it can hold for so many centuries, a small respite will do no harm."

The water seemed to flow from Violet's stomach to her extremities, where it replenished some of what she'd lost in her battle. "What do we do now?" she asked. "How can we regain our strength most quickly, Leo? Remember I still need to find out what happened to my father?"

"I know you are worried, my love, but we must wait and heal. I do not think it will be wise for us to try to return to the city for some time. We are weak and must replenish our strength."

Though she wanted to argue, she knew it was pointless. *You can't even walk. How would you shuffle through the desert… and then across the whole city, since Azaan and his car are no longer available?*

"I suppose we must eat the dates first. They are very nutritious and will sustain us until we can set snares for the desert hares. Once we feel a bit stronger, we can explore for more vegetables as well. That, along with rest, water and time is what we need. I fear it will not be quick. We are both dangerously depleted."

Violet frowned, but she knew he was right.

All told, it took a full ten days for Violet and Leontios to recover from their ordeal enough to risk the walk across the desert to Cairo. Though the heat had broken while they recuperated, with highs only in the seventies during the day, they still opted to travel at night, and though the moon had waned considerably, Violet was now able to channel its light, and she glowed like a lantern.

Periodically, Leontios would pause in their walking to point out a new landmark. She could practically see his tattoos changing to accommodate his new information.

"Good thing you have an excellent sense of direction," she commented. "I don't think we'll get that lost again."

"We were never lost, Violet," he asked. "I always knew where we were. I only was not sure about the gate."

Violet sighed.

At the end of the night, they made it back to the

tavern and slipped into the room. Its modernity assaulted Violet's senses like a jarring noise.

"I'm shocked you made it back," the innkeeper said, staring at them both as though he'd seen a ghost. "What with everything that's happened."

"What happened?" Violet demanded.

"There's been outright rebellion," a man shouted over a plate of breakfast. "Demonstrations and marches all over the city. They say the women in their veils are marching alongside the men!"

"I hear the countryside is worse," another man bellowed.

Violet shook her head. "We have so far to go."

"Where?"

"The Shepheard Hotel," she said. "I think my father is there."

"I can give you a ride," the bartender said.

"I do not enjoy riding in cars," Leontios said.

The bartender chuckled despite the tension in the room. "If you rode on the back of Azaan's death machine, I'm not surprised. I have something you'll like much better."

Better turned out to be a wagon pulled by a sleepy, gentle mule. It didn't move them quickly through the streets, but it was more comfortable. Violet leaned against Leontios's shoulder and let her eyes drift closed to the rhythmic clopping of hooves and the gentle squeaking of wheels.

She started awake when the wagon pulled to a

halt outside their destination. "How much do I owe you?" Violet asked sleepily.

He shook his head. "Stop by for a beer when you come back my way. You can tell me some wild tale of your adventures."

"Thank you."

They stepped inside the dining room to see Ennis and Bilbrey seated at a table, sipping tea.

"Hello," Violet said softly as she approached them. "Sorry to disturb you."

"Where have ye been, lass?" Ennis demanded.

"Away," Violet replied. "An emergency arose, and we had to deal with it immediately. Sounds like there have been some emergencies here as well."

"Oh, yes," Bilbrey agreed, eyes glowing with excitement. "We'll see some action now."

"That action is people fighting for their homeland," Ennis reminded him. "It's not good form to be excited about oppressing them."

"You're an old lady, Ennis," Bilbrey said, shoving a bit of cake into his mouth.

"Was there ever any word from my father?" Violet asked, turning their attention away from their philosophical differences.

"Aye," Ennis said, and his already somber face turned sorrowful.

Violet's stomach dropped.

"The bastards killed him," Bilbrey blurted.

Ennis kicked him under the table. "Learn some

tact, man. Ma'am, he was badly injured in the derailment and was not able to get help quickly enough. I heard he never regained consciousness, so I don't think he suffered at all. Someone will want you to decide what to do with the body, and soon. Do you need me to help you make arrangements for your return to America?"

Violet bit her lip. "I don't know what my plans are just now." She exhaled a shaky breath, and Leontios's arm snaked around her waist. The two men stared.

Beyond caring what they thought, she asked one last question. "Did any of the luggage come this way?"

Bilbrey nodded. "It should be in your room. Lucky your trunk has your name on it. And that you reserved two weeks at the hotel!"

Violet nodded and let Leontios lead her up the stairs. With the heat broken, the room no longer remained uncomfortably stuffy. Violet sank onto the bed. It felt strange and lumpy after so many nights in Skeon. Every ache she'd endured for the last ten days awoke and began to torture her again. While her body hurt, her heart felt numb. Her mind buzzed.

"He's gone," she said softly. "Poor Father. My poor, poor father."

Leontios hugged her and urged her down onto the soft mattress, where he cuddled her against his chest. "I wish I could have met him," he told her.

"He wouldn't have liked you," she admitted, stunned that she could converse normally after receiving such a painful blow. *I must be in shock. That won't last forever.* "You're everything he's not in favor of. But he would have accepted you because you're my choice. What do I do now?"

"Well, you may want to spend some time grieving in this room. When you are ready, you must make arrangements to lay him to rest according to the customs of your people. Then, you must decide how you wish to proceed. I hope that you will stay with me, in Skeon. Perhaps it would be wise to retreat there as I have no wish to see you embroiled in this unrest. Of course, you might wish to return to Pitts-burgh? Was that not the name?"

"It is the name," Violet agreed, "and I have no desire to go back. While I have an inheritance coming, and there's a house to sell and various other legal matters to attend to, I'm sure they can be handled from here—and if you think the modern world is strange, just wait until I show you a telephone. You'll be amazed. But we'll do all that eventually. When things settle down. I'm not in a rush. We only need a few small, inexpensive items to equip Skeon for long-term life. If you'll have me, I'd prefer to go back home—our home."

She swallowed and inhaled a shaking breath.

"We both have a lot of feelings we've suppressed too long, and if we're not careful, like the crystal, they may rupture. But I'd rather not do it here. Can't we just… just prepare ourselves as quickly as the situation allows and then go home to do it?"

He gave her an approving look.

She returned a pinched smile. Her face felt so tight, it seemed as though her skin would crack. "The only question is, how do we get all this… stuff through the desert? It's too heavy to carry.

"I suppose we will have to find someone with pack animals to help us."

Violet raised an eyebrow. "You would allow people to know where Skeon is? Now, in the midst of a rebellion?"

"Perhaps we could borrow them?" he suggested.

She nodded. "A wise plan. Or buy them, maybe. I like animals. I wouldn't mind having one or two. I think… I think I'd like to get started. I'll wait until we get home to fall apart."

Rising, she opened her trunk and removed additional ammunition for her derringer. "There. That's as prepared as I can be for unrest. I hope I don't have to use it."

"As do I," Leontios agreed. "I would like these people one day to be my neighbors. It will not be an auspicious start if we must defend ourselves against a mob."

"Then we had better get started right away," Violet suggested, rising stiffly to her feet. Her body ached. "Maybe the hotel employees can point us in the right direction."

"Perhaps."

"Leontios," Violet said, "Um, while we're procuring supplies, you should look into getting a new book. Your old one was too full already. There's almost no skin left on you that isn't marked."

"An excellent idea, my love," he replied. "And perhaps, in time, you will allow me to place your life force into it. Then, you too will not age or die. I do not think I could bear to lose you."

"I think that would be just fine," Violet said. Pushing down her sorrow and lethargy until a more appropriate time, Violet took her beloved's hand, and together they left the hotel room, intent on beginning a new adventure.

Their future together.

AUTHOR'S NOTE

*T*hank you for reading this historical paranormal romance. I hope you have enjoyed trekking through the desert with Violet and Leontios as much as I enjoyed writing about them. They are a truly special couple, and it was a blast telling their story.

If you notice some differences between ACTUAL Pittsburg and /or Egypt, I pray you will suspend your disbelief. Liberties were taken to suit the story. This is not meant to represent pictorial reality of either location, but rather provide grounding for an otherwise fantastical story.

If you enjoyed the story, please leave a review. Even a simple "I liked it," will suffice. Readers and reviewers make it possible for authors to continue writing. Your feedback is greatly appreciated.

If you would like to contact me, I'm available by email at simonebeaudelaireauthor@hotmail.com or through my website at http://simonebeaudelaire.com. Or through the Next Chapter website at https://www.nextchapter.pub/authors/simone-beaudelaire-romance-author. I always appreciate hearing from readers, so don't be afraid to reach out!

Love always,
Simone Beaudelaire

ABOUT THE AUTHOR

In the world of the written word, Simone Beaudelaire strives for technical excellence while advancing a worldview in which the sacred and the sensual blend into stories of people whose relationships are founded in faith but are no less passionate for it. Unapologetically explicit, yet undeniably classy, Beaudelaire's 20+ novels aim to make readers think, cry, pray… and get a little hot and bothered.

In real life, the author's alter-ego teaches composition at a community college in a small western Kansas town, where she lives with her four children, three cats, and husband—fellow author Edwin Stark.

As both romance writer and academic, Beaudelaire devotes herself to promoting the rhetorical value of the romance in hopes of overcoming the stigma associated with literature's biggest female-centered genre.

BOOKS BY SIMONE BEAUDELAIRE

When the Music Ends (The Hearts in Winter Chronicles
Book 1)

When the Words are Spoken (The Hearts in Winter
Chronicles Book 2)

Caroline's Choice (The Hearts in Winter Chronicles
Book 3)

When the Heart Heals (The Hearts in Winter Chronicles
Book 4)

The Naphil's Kiss

Blood Fever

Polar Heat

Xaman (with Edwin Stark)

Darkness Waits (with Edwin Stark)

Watching Over the Watcher

Baylee Breaking

Amor Maldito: Romantic Tragedies from Tejano Folklore

Keeping Katerina (The Victorians Book 1)

Devin's Dilemma (The Victorians Book 2)

Colin's Conundrum (The Victorians Book 3)

High Plains Promise (Love on the High Plains Book 2)

High Plains Heartbreak (Love on the High Plains Book 3)

High Plains Passion (Love on the High Plains Book 4)

Devilfire (American Hauntings Book 1)

Saving Sam (The Wounded Warriors Book 1 with J.M. Northup)

Justifying Jack (The Wounded Warriors Book 2 with J.M. Northup)

Making Mike (The Wounded Warriors Book 3 with J.M Northup)

Si tu m'Aimes (If you Love me)

Where the Wind Blows

You Within Me
ISBN: 978-4-86747-272-9
Large Print

Published by
Next Chapter
1-60-20 Minami-Otsuka
170-0005 Toshima-Ku, Tokyo
+818035793528

4th October 2021

Lightning Source UK Ltd.
Milton Keynes UK
UKHW011845020622
403916UK00002B/87